All in December

BEC BENSON

ISBN: 978-1-968356-02-6 (Print)

ISBN: 978-1-968356-03-3 (Kindle)

Book Cover: Amimbia

Editor: Raven Quill Editing

Content Warnings

This is a low-angst, feel-good winter romance, but it does include mentions of divorce, homophobia, an unsupportive family and ex-wife, and consensual degradation and mild exhibitionism in sexual contexts.

You're never too old, too late, or too much.

CHAPTER 1

Caleb

"We'll do one more run, then we can stop for lunch, okay?"

Sam nods at me, breathing a little heavy from the last trail we just skied down, but I know that won't slow him down. He has that endless kid energy I can't quite keep up with anymore at thirty-four. I smile at him, resigned to the fact that over-priced chicken tenders are in my immediate future.

We shuffle forward in the lift line, skis clanging awkwardly against each other as we merge with the busy Saturday crowd. I nudge Sam gently, steering us toward the four-person lane.

"Is it just you two?" a deep voice behind me asks.

I turn, and for a second, I forget how cold my fingers are or that my nose is half frozen because *damn*. Even though most of his face is hidden behind a neck gaiter and a helmet, the man behind me is stunning. He's a few inches taller than me, and his bright blue eyes are visible through his clear goggle lenses.

"Uh, yep," I say, quickly, suddenly feeling nervous even though riding the lift with strangers is a very common thing.

He lifts a hand, gesturing to the boy next to him. "Cool. We'll hop on with you."

It's only then that I notice there's a boy who looks to be about Sam's age standing quietly at his side. His helmet is slightly crooked, and he's got a bright blue coat on.

I move to the outside so Sam can be in the middle, and the two boys now stand next to each other as the line moves closer and closer to the chair lift.

"I'm Nash," the man says, reaching his hand out to me with a big smile.

"Caleb." I smile back and remind myself to breathe.

While I've ridden the lift with many strangers over the years, people don't typically introduce themselves—especially not before getting on—and no one has ever shaken my hand before like he does. It's awkward doing it over our kids and with gloves and ski poles, but I kind of like it.

It's our turn, and the lift operator waves us forward. Sam scrambles ahead, and Nash's son quickly follows before he and I ski forward to wait. We plop down when the chair comes around, and the lift jerks upward as it ascends the mountain.

For a moment, it's quiet as we pull down the bar and get settled into the chair. Well, apart from a few little grunts, groans, and clanging of equipment while all four of us try to adjust our skis on the foot rest and get our poles situated.

"How's your day been?" Nash asks, turning his head toward me, looking over the boys.

"Good," I begin. "Early start, but he's been loving it." I nod toward Sam, who's talking to the other boy.

"Awesome. We drove in late last night. He was supposed to be with his mom this weekend, but she had plans to go holiday shopping. When he groaned about it, she offered to just take his sister, Emma, and said I could take him skiing instead. So now we're doing a boys' weekend on the mountain."

"That sounds better than shopping for sure." I laugh.

"Dad, can we do that soon? I want to stay up here," Sam interrupts.

"Yeah, of course," I promise. "We can look when we get home and plan a trip soon."

"Cool," he says, satisfied, turning back to his own conversation.

"Obviously, we're only up for the day," I chuckle over the top of the boys' heads.

Nash smiles at me softly, and his expression looks so full of understanding. "That's usually all we can do, too. But it's nice to stay this weekend, especially with the storm coming in."

I nod at him before my eyes drift out over the massive Colorado mountains ahead of us. There are jagged snowy peaks that cut across the gray sky, and the slopes below are lined with dark evergreens dusted white.

"Do you live in Denver?" I ask.

"Yeah, we do. What about you?"

"Same here," I nod. "I love that skiing here for the day is even an option." I'm not used to being so chatty on the lift, but there's something about him that's drawing me in, and it's not just those bright, glacier-water blue eyes of his. "How old is your son?" I ask.

"Benji's nine. How about yours?"

"Sam's eight. It's cool they're close in age, probably why

they seem to be getting along so well already," I add, still wanting to keep this conversation going.

He smiles again, and it suddenly feels unseasonably warm for such a chilly December day. And it's cold—the kind of cold that's sharp enough to sting your lungs. Yet his smile makes my chest do that stupid flutter thing I thought I'd never feel again at this age.

"Maybe they'll end up ski buddies by the end of the day," Nash suggests.

The end of the day? Is he implying that we'll be spending the day together? My chest flutters again, somehow more aggressively this time, at the implication his words hold. I lick my lips before raking the bottom one between my teeth, trying to hold back an overly telling smile. I can already tell I'd really like to spend the day with him. It's impossible not to overthink his words, but I'd kind of like to be ski buddies with him, too. Or… whatever the grown-up version of that is.

"Seems like we're heading that way." I laugh as I listen to the boys' conversation evolve into their favorite trails on the mountain.

The chair sways slightly as it pauses for a moment, and I glance at Nash again, trying not to stare. It's a challenge, though, with how handsome he is, with his bright smile, olive skin, and dark brown strands of hair sticking out from under his helmet. There's a familiarity to him I can't place—not in a I-know-you way, but in a I-get-you kind of way. It's evident in how he watches his son and seems to find joy in the shared moments like these with him.

Single dad radar, maybe. Or maybe just loneliness recognizing itself in someone else, even though he doesn't appear to be lonely at all.

It's been a long time since I felt a genuine connection with someone, and between work and Sam, my time is limited. I want to date again and fall in love, but I don't know when I'll be able to find the time, let alone my person.

As we approach the summit, the sky is darker and the snow falls heavier. It's always fascinated me how the base and the peak can have such different weather, even though they're only a few thousand feet apart in elevation.

"Storm's rolling in," Nash says with a big smile. "Hopefully it means fresh snow tomorrow."

I nod, shifting my goggles into place, thinking about how much I suddenly wish we were staying the night. Nash keeps mentioning a storm, and maybe I should've looked at the weather more closely before we drove up this morning. I knew it was going to snow, but I have no idea how much.

Maybe we should head out after the lunch I'd already promised Sam, even though I already hate that idea.

As we approach the drop zone, the chair slows just enough for us to all slide off, skis scraping against packed powder. We glide out of the way of the next riders and turn toward the trail on the right.

"You wanna ski down together?" Nash asks.

My stomach flutters once again because he actually meant what he said on the chairlift. He wasn't just being friendly—he meant it—and someone following through on what they said they'd do? That's a major green flag for me.

"Sounds fun. You wanna do that, bud?" I ask Sam, even though I'm pretty sure I already know the answer, since he and Benji are still talking by themselves.

"Yes!" he shouts and turns to Benji. "Race you to the bottom?"

"You're on!" Benji replies, and I really hope no one ends up with a twisted ankle.

They push off, skiing down the mountain, and I can't help but laugh at their enthusiasm.

"Ready?" Nash asks, and I give him a quick nod.

He follows behind the boys, and I take off a moment later, leaning into the slope. The air bites at my cheeks as we pick up speed, flying down a wide trail lined with snowy evergreens. I've always thought that certain snows make the trees look like they've been spray-painted white, and today's one of those days.

The trail we're on is labeled as a blue with only a few steep parts, and it's a run Sam and I have done countless times.

Sam's laugh carries up the mountain to me as he tucks his little body forward to try to beat Benji, but Benji keeps up, cutting quick, tight turns behind him. I'm just glad neither of them is trying to straight-line it down the mountain. The last thing they need is to pick up speed too quickly and end up hurt in the ski patrol's sled.

Nash and I are still behind them, letting them have their fun.

"They're having the time of their lives today, huh?" he calls over the wind, glancing sideways at me as we hit a flatter stretch.

"You can say that again." I laugh. "He's definitely having more fun now than he was with just me."

He chuckles. "Yeah, Benji too. He loves to show off when he's got friends around. He terrifies me every time he leaves the ground."

I motion toward the boys as Benji skis over a small bump, getting a couple of inches of air at most, and Sam follows, doing the same. "Like that?"

"Exactly like that." He laughs easily.

I don't remember the last time I felt this at ease talking to someone new, especially another dad. Usually, it feels like forced, awkward small talk. Or trying to figure out what to say without oversharing, yet still saying enough to fit in with the other parents. But with Nash, it's been surprisingly easy, almost like we've somehow already skipped a few steps to make it to the fun and comfortable part of friendship.

By the time we reach the base, Sam's cheeks are red, and he's grinning from ear to ear. He turns to me with wide eyes. "Did you see that jump, Dad? I got so much air!"

"You did," I agree, even if he barely left the ground. "I also saw my life flash before my eyes."

He grins and turns to Benji. "Wanna do that one again after lunch?"

Benji nods with a huge smile on his face. "Definitely!"

Nash pulls off his gloves, letting them hang from his wrists. "You guys eating at the lodge now?"

"Yeah, I promised Sam we'd stop after one more run right before you guys hopped in line with us," I say as I watch the boys take off their skis, Benji already moving like he's coming with us. "Sam's on a strict diet of overpriced chicken tenders and hot chocolate."

Nash chuckles. "Benji, too. Must be something they worked into the ski school curriculum all those years ago."

"I think you might be right about that," I joke. "You guys want to eat together? It's always hard finding a table, and the boys seem to be getting along... but no pressure if you've got other plans," I add, because I don't want him to feel obligated.

Nash looks down at Benji, who's nodding enthusiastically, then back at me. "Yeah, we'd love to."

"Cool." I unclip my boots from my skis and try to be cool

about this, but I'm more nervous than I'd like to admit with this ridiculous urge to impress Nash.

After we line our skis up on the rack outside, Nash pushes the door open, and a rush of warm air hits us the second we step inside. We stomp the snow off our boots, unzip our jackets, and make our way further into the large lodge. It's less of a cozy cabin and more of a busy food court with multiple stations to pick from, tables packed shoulder to shoulder, and people everywhere.

I wasn't exaggerating when I said it's hard to find a spot. But lucky for us, there's an empty table by the oversized wood-burning fireplace tucked in the corner that we manage to snag.

Nash and I both hand the boys money, and judging by the look Nash gives me, we're both thinking the same thing: Let them pick what they want, then eat whatever they inevitably leave behind.

I set my gloves and helmet on the table before dropping into the wooden chair, and a sigh escapes me. "Why does skiing make you feel like you've been hit by a truck, even when you're having fun?"

Nash laughs as he takes off his helmet. "Because it's secretly a full-body workout disguised as a good time."

Usually, I'd laugh because he's correct, but right now, I'm trying to pick up my jaw. Nash is hot. This is the first time I'm seeing him without his helmet and goggles on and… holy hell, I don't even have words.

His brown hair is a sweaty mess with damp curls plastered around the edge of his forehead. My eyes trace the movement of his hand as he reaches up to run his fingers through the strands like he's trying to bring them back to life. His cheeks are flushed red from the cold, and his jawline is coated in stubble. He's the whole stupidly attractive package, and I quickly look away, pretending to search for the boys before I start drooling.

"Uh," he starts, drawing my attention back to him. I must've done a bad job of hiding my disbelief at how handsome he is, though, because he's looking at me with a confused expression. "Everything okay?" he questions, probably from my strange response to his joke.

My cheeks heat more at Nash calling me out, but my god, how am I supposed to act normal when the hottest man I've ever seen is sitting across the table from me? "Yep. Totally. Just trying to see where Sam went," I say, shaking my head and blinking to try to snap out of it.

But all that does is make me realize Nash is also seeing me for the first time right now, and I'm a sweaty mess who can't pull it off nearly as well as he does.

He leans back in his chair, arms stretched casually over the backrest of the empty one next to him, and smirks. Fucking smirks. Like he wasn't already radiating hot single dad energy all over this ski lodge.

I'm so fucked.

He's got to know what he's doing to me. My cheeks are still hot, and the tips of my ears are burning now, but at least I managed to pick up my jaw and blink.

Thankfully, Sam and Benji return with their trays of chicken tenders and fries, and what I'm assuming is a cup of hot chocolate, interrupting us before I can embarrass myself further.

"Make sure you don't eat yourself into a food coma." Nash laughs as he warns Benji, and probably Sam. "We've still got a whole afternoon of skiing still ahead of us."

They both nod at him, and I smile at the fact that Sam seems to feel comfortable around the two of them already.

The three of them talk while I try to stop sneaking glances at Nash, but he's making it hard. He's funny, and present, and he looks at Benji like he hung the moon—and yes, he's the most attractive man I've ever seen.

It's a dangerous combination, and it's making me want to explore all my quiet desires for the very first time.

CHAPTER 2
Nash

C aleb is sexy as hell.

I thought he was attractive when I first saw him in the lift line, though I don't think he noticed me. Still, I took the chance to ask if he wanted to ride together since he seemed to be with his son, too.

As soon as we started talking, I didn't want to stop. There's this quiet, slightly shy energy about him, but I get the sense there's more underneath it. It already feels like something I want to figure out.

Now that he's free of his ski gear, I've confirmed I was right—he's definitely attractive. His cheeks are still flushed from the cold, and there's a slight sheen of sweat on his forehead. He's a few inches shorter than me, with short, messy, dirty-blond hair, and pale blue eyes with hazel flecks that catch the light when he looks up.

He's glanced at me a couple of times, and I can't tell if he's feeling what I'm feeling or if I'm imagining it. There's just something about him that's pulling me in.

Dating has been a complete shit show since my ex-wife

and I divorced four years ago—and by shit show, I mean it's barely happened. I've dated a couple of women and a few men since then, and every time, I've wanted to teleport myself home mid-conversation. They were all fine. Kind, mostly. But I could tell they weren't for me.

I've also stopped agreeing to blind dates. Especially the ones where well-meaning friends tried to set me up with their "sweet gay coworker" once I told them I'm bi. Just because someone's also into men does not mean we're a match made in queer heaven. I don't understand why straight people think that's the only qualifier. Like "Oh! You're both attracted to men? And breathing? It's fate!" when it's most definitely not.

Needless to say, I've stopped dating altogether. It's been easier to focus on Benji and Emma and work. There's far less disappointment that way. But now Caleb is sitting across from me, talking to our sons, and I'm feeling a buzz in my chest that hasn't been there in years. I'm warm and curious and desperate for more time with him, and we haven't even parted ways yet.

"Dad, I'm full," Benji complains, pushing his tray away.

"Me too," Sam echoes, and Caleb and I both laugh.

Without saying anything, we both start picking off the boys' trays, finishing what they couldn't as our lunch.

"Alright, ready to go back out?" I ask once we've cleared the table.

Everyone nods, and we hit the bathroom then layer back up with our coats, gloves, helmets, and goggles.

Outside, the snow's falling steadier now, white flakes catching on our goggles and dusting our jackets as we grab our skis from the rack. The air has an extra layer of chill to it now with the wind, but there's nothing better than skiing while the snow's still falling.

Once we've all grabbed our skis from the rack, we make our way to the lift line. We agree on one more run to start and then to see how everyone's feeling afterward. It's only midday, but my legs are already tired, and I know I'm going to feel it tomorrow. Still, I'm not quitting now, not in front of the kids, and definitely not in front of Caleb.

Not when this day feels worth holding onto.

Sam and Benji are talking a mile a minute now with their post-lunch high. They're feeding off each other's energy, talking about who'd win a fight between a bear and a moose, and getting louder by the sentence.

It's hard not to smile watching Benji, clearly having a great day with his new friend.

Since the trip was a little last minute, none of his friends from school were free to come. I'd been worried it might be a lonely day for him, but now he's beaming. Introducing myself to Caleb might've been the best decision I've made in a long time.

"Do you make it up to ski a lot?" I ask as we near the line.

He shrugs. "We try to come around ten days or so each season. I used to come more before Sam. Now it's mostly short trips, whatever we can fit on weekends and school breaks."

"Same," I say. "Benji's with me half the time, along with his sister, Emma. I always try to cram the good stuff into the time we get, but occasionally I'll come up here without the two of them."

He nods at me, and for a moment, we just look at each other. It feels like we both understand the responsibility of raising our kids. He hasn't said anything about his relationship status or Sam's mom, and the desire to know is clawing at me.

I want to ask. I want to know if he's single, too, and if we have a chance.

But it's far too soon for those kinds of thoughts, so I clamp my mouth shut as the chairlift swings around and scoops us up.

Once we're settled, the boys are back at it like they never stopped.

"Benji," Sam says, adjusting his goggles. "If you could have any superpower, what would it be?"

Benji doesn't even hesitate. "Teleportation. Then I could go anywhere I want, whenever I want and not have to sit in traffic or ask Dad."

I snort. "Wow. Harsh."

Caleb chuckles beside me. "I mean… he's got a point. Denver traffic is brutal."

"Traitor," I mutter with a smirk and a wink because he's not wrong.

Sam turns his little body to look at his dad on the other side of him next. "What about you guys? If you were a superhero?"

Caleb shrugs. "Flight, probably. Seems efficient."

Benji looks at me next, expectantly. "What about you, Dad?"

"I'd want to be invisible. Maybe I'd get some peace and quiet, and get out of driving your butt around in traffic," I say, smiling big at Benji.

That gets a laugh out of all of them, including Benji.

I wipe off the snow that's piling up on his jacket as we're riding up the lift. It's coming down heavier now, and my mind immediately goes to Caleb.

"Feels like we're about to get buried," I say, turning toward him. "You think you'll be able to get out tonight?"

He gives me a concerned look, as if we just shared the same thought. "I was just questioning my choices. I didn't realize the snow was going to hit so early. I should've looked at the weather when we were in the lodge. This feels like poor planning on my part."

"I can always see if the lodge we're staying at has an open room when we get back down," I say, secretly hoping they have the conjoining room next to mine open so we can keep hanging out.

He gives me a quick smile and the tension slightly eases from his face. "Probably not a bad idea, thanks for thinking of doing that."

"Of course." Even if part of it's selfish, I still want them safe. Driving back to Denver in the snow is anything but.

When we hit the top of the run, the boys immediately start making their way back down. Sam is yelling something about racing again, and just like earlier, we ski behind them. Caleb is a good skier; he's confident but not showy—not that I'd expect him to be, that doesn't seem like his style, and it's not like many people are show-offs at our age. Instead, he keeps an eye on Sam, just like I do for Benji. I've noticed the way he looks at his son with a mix of joy, exhaustion, and awe, and I know that feeling down to my bones.

By the time we hit the base, I'm sure I don't want our time together to end, which, even as outgoing and extroverted as I am, is odd for me. I'm not typically the "let's spend more time with strangers type," but this doesn't feel like that. It doesn't feel like we're strangers at all.

Lucky for me, the boys beg for a few more runs, and Caleb must not be that concerned about the weather, so we keep going in the fresh snow until we're all completely worn out. Skiing in fresh powder always makes my legs extra tired, but it's a hell of a lot of fun, so it's worth it.

The snow has picked up even more by the time we unclip our skis, and I pull out my phone to check the time and the weather app. It's worse than I was expecting as an alert flashes across the weather app on my home screen:

WINTER STORM WARNING IN EFFECT UNTIL
TOMORROW AT 11 A.M. TRAVEL STRONGLY
DISCOURAGED.

I turn my phone to show Caleb. "I'm gonna call the lodge now for you," I tell him. Looking back, we probably should have done this five runs ago when we first talked about it, but we were having too much fun.

He exhales, a puff of white breath in the cold air. "Thank you. That'd be great. Shit, I should have done this at lunch."

"I was just thinking the same thing. I'll be right back," I say as I step away to dial the number, waiting for the hotel to pick up.

"Summit Lodge, this is Ashley. How can I help you?"

"Hi, Ashley, do you have any rooms available tonight?" I check.

I hear her sigh like she's about to give me bad news. "We're completely booked for the night. The storm sold us out quickly. Sorry about that."

Well, there goes the joint room dream.

I glance back at Caleb, who's also checking his phone, all while Sam and Benji keep chatting without a care in the world. I could call other hotels to see if they have openings or offer to look on Airbnb for him, but I have another idea I like far better.

"No problem," I say. "We're all set, thanks."

"Okay, goodbye, sir."

"Bye." I hang up and walk back over, already mentally rehearsing how to make what I'm about to say not sound weird.

Caleb looks up as I approach. "Any luck?"

"No." I shake my head. "They're totally sold out with the storm."

He mutters something under his breath, rubbing a hand over his face, and the desire that comes over me to help ease his stress feels like instinct. I *want* to help him in this situation, not only to spend more time with him but because I want to make his life better, easier. I want to solve his problems; let him know he can lean on me.

And I've only known him for hours.

"But," I add, "Our room has two queen beds. You and Sam are welcome to stay with us."

His eyes lift to mine, and I can see the hesitation there, probably debating between not wanting to impose but not feeling safe driving home. He looks to Sam, who is nodding his head, and then back to me with a gulp.

"You're sure?" he asks, already sounding like he wants to say yes, but needs the out if he's overstepping. His hesitation is adorable in this moment, when all I really want is to pull him into me and tell him I've got him.

"Completely sure. There's plenty of room, and Benji'll be thrilled, won't ya, bud?" I ask, and his smile grows even bigger.

"Yes, please stay!" he shouts. "Then we can ski again tomorrow! There's going to be so much fresh snow!"

I laugh, but Caleb still looks unsure. "Come here for a

second," I say, tilting my head and stepping forward. He follows as we put a few feet between us and the boys.

"If you're uncomfortable staying the night, I completely understand. There's no pressure, and I'm sorry I didn't ask you away from the kids," I say quietly. "But if you're only hesitant because you're worried about being a burden, don't be. I'd really like you to stay, and I know Benji would too. He was bummed that none of his friends from school could come up this weekend, and he and Sam seem to really be getting along well. It'll be great," I promise, hoping I'll be able to convince him that we should definitely spend more time together, because no part of me wants him to go home tonight.

Caleb huffs out a small laugh, the tension softening as he looks back over his shoulder at our kids. "Yeah, okay. Sam already asked if we could ski with you guys again tomorrow when we weren't even planning to come back tomorrow. I think he'd like to stay, and besides, driving home in this snow would be a nightmare."

It's laughable how happy that makes me—to know he agreed and that his son likes mine enough to want to spend more time together. I should probably play it cool since I have no idea if he's single, or into men, but I'm grinning like an idiot at the opportunity for more time with him.

God, I really hope he's single and into men.

And feeling even a fraction of what I'm feeling for him.

"Great," I exclaim. "We're staying at the Summit Lodge. We'll head over, and you two can meet us there."

"Thanks, Nash."

"It's no problem at all," I say, going to turn away to help Benji and get out of my gear when I realize I don't even have a way to contact him. "Actually, put your number in my phone. I'll text you what room we're in."

He sends himself a message from my phone, and I feel like a teenager again, about to text my crush for the first time.

CHAPTER 3
Caleb

O kay, okay. This is *fine*.

It's not weird or a big deal. People share hotel rooms all the time. In movies. On ski trips. In, like... survival situations. Which this kind of is, right?

There *is* a snowstorm, and knowing how Colorado works, it's very likely that the road will close if it hasn't already from everyone trying to get back and sliding into each other. I can't take that risk with Sam, especially when it was hard enough to drive from the base of the mountain to the hotel. It took ten minutes when it probably should have taken two, and the last thing I want is to multiply that for an almost two-hour drive. It's simply not worth it.

Tonight is just two dads trying to make it through the night with their sons and their dignity intact.

Sam is thrilled about the sleepover invitation. He, of course, is totally unfazed by the fact that we're about to share a hotel room with strangers. Well, technically not strangers. I know Nash and Benji's names. And the fact that Nash's eyes are crazy blue, and he has really nice hands, and he looks unfairly good in ski gear, and I am undeniably attracted to him.

I'm trying to remain calm about this situation, but I feel like I'm coming across as awkward. I can't tell if Nash is flirting with me or is even into men, and I have no idea *how* to flirt with men, especially since I've never been good at it in the first place with women.

My ex really did a number on my self-esteem when she left me.

"Dad, did you hear me?" Sam cuts through my thoughts. "Benji said there's a heated pool at the hotel! Can we go? Please?"

"Yeah, bud," I say, trying to pull my head out of my ass. "Let's just get to the room first, okay?"

The whole way over here, he's told me he had the best day ever—making a new friend, skiing until he could barely stand, and now he gets to have a sleepover in a hotel during a snowstorm in the mountains. He's over the moon. And I'm trying not to overthink the fact that I'm about to share a hotel room with the most attractive man I've ever met. A man I talked to for the first time this morning.

I'm happy for Sam. Really. He deserves this kind of joy. But my brain is running a mile a minute overthinking every awkward possibility—what if I snore? What if I have to pee in the middle of the night? What if I accidentally say something embarrassing and Nash regrets his invite?

I need to pull it together. It's just one night. Given that it's with a very kind, very charming man who somehow makes me feel more seen than I have in years is irrelevant.

Damn it, I'm doomed.

When we pull into the snow-covered parking lot, I text Nash that we're here and grab the bag I always pack which, luckily, has a change of clothes. It's not like we ever actually change after skiing, but I always throw it in the car just in case. Today that "just in case" mentality really paid off, otherwise we'd be stuck in the same sweaty clothes all night.

"Come on, Dad!" Sam yells impatiently as I finish up at the car.

"Alright, I'm ready," I say, hitting the lock button before putting my hand back in my coat. It's absolutely freezing out here, and despite how nervous I am about sharing the hotel room, I really am relieved we don't need to drive home in this weather.

Nash texted me the room number before we left the mountain parking lot, but when we walk inside the lobby, he's there waiting for us with a big smile on his face.

"Hey! Glad you agreed to stay, the roads are already crazy," he greets, and I'm even happier to be here now that he seems genuinely excited to see us... and somehow slightly more nervous.

The hotel's nice, in that slightly outdated, rustic kind of way. It was probably the pinnacle of mountain luxury when the resort first opened, and it hasn't changed much since then. Wood beams stretch across the ceiling, and a big stone fireplace crackles in the center of the room, surrounded by worn brown leather chairs. There's a lobby bar tucked into the corner that looks busy, likely with people taking advantage of being snowed in.

"Happy we're staying, thanks again. Lead the way." I gesture to Nash.

He walks toward the elevator, and I can't help but notice how his hair is still a bit damp from his helmet sweat, curling a little at the ends in a way that makes me want to run my fingers through it.

Get it together, Caleb. You've known this man for less than a day.

For someone who's never been with a man, my imagination is having no trouble picturing all the things I'd like to do with him. I keep cycling between feeling intrigued and flustered, and I have no idea if he's feeling anything at all. He could just be a nice person who's offering a helping hand.

That's probably all it is.

Once the elevator dings and opens on the floor we're staying on, Sam and I follow Nash down the long hallway to the room we're sharing. Nash opens the door, and the room is rustic with a mountain-themed feel, but what my eyes get stuck on is the two beds in the room. They're so close together with only an end table to separate them, and I gulp at how close Nash and I will be sleeping. I don't know why I didn't think about this earlier when he invited us. Of course they have a standard hotel room with two beds. I'm pretty sure he told me that but I was too overwhelmed to process it.

"This is awesome." Sam grins as soon as we're in the room.

"Can we share a bed?" Benji asks Nash before I even put my bag down, and I freeze.

My brain short-circuits because kids are so damn direct, and I have no idea what to do right now.

Does Nash want to share a bed with me? Is that something he's even considered? Is it going to be weird? It's going to be weird. We just met. My face is burning hot, and my palms are sweaty. I've never felt this flustered in my life.

Oh god, why did I sign us up to share a room with them?

It's been all of sixty seconds and he's already going to regret this invitation.

"Yeah! Can we, Dad? Please?" Sam shouts with bubbling excitement because, of course, he needs to pile on the pressure, even if it's completely unintentional.

I glance at Nash, eyebrows raised, hoping he'll take the lead here, because honestly, I have no idea what the right move is. I hate being the one to make decisions that involve someone else's comfort, especially when that someone isn't Sam. This whole situation is already pushing the boundaries of what I know how to navigate, and that's the most challenging part of being a single parent—always single-handedly having to be the one to make every decision. There are so many moments I wish I could just give up control and have someone tell me what to do instead of constantly second-guessing myself.

"Well…" I start, still unsure how to answer. That is, until I look over at Nash, who is smiling at me.

"Do you care?" he checks.

"No. Not at all," I say far too fast. "It's totally fine." I lie because nothing about this is fine. How are we going to sleep in the same bed together? What if we touch each other, or I roll into him and try to cuddle him? It's been a long time since I've shared a bed with anyone. Oh god, what if I get a boner? What if I wake up and my hard dick is pressed into his ass? Why did we agree to this? This was the most foolish plan I've ever had.

"Alright, great," Nash says, nodding toward the boys who are already debating who gets what side. "And this way we don't have to deal with them yelling across the room to each other."

"True," I huff before I swallow down all my nerves. Not

only am I sharing a hotel room with the most attractive man I've ever laid eyes on, but now, due to our children, I'm sharing a bed with him. A bed!

"Exactly, works better for all of us." Nash smiles easily, probably completely fine with this.

"Yep, cool," I nervously agree.

"Cool," he echoes.

The kids don't even notice the awkward tension because they're too busy arranging pillows... or something. I'm really not sure what they're doing since I've managed to block them and their entire conversation out of my mind to spiral over my own struggles. I've accepted I'm not winning any Dad of the Year awards based on my behavior right now.

Unsure of what else to do, I pick our bag up to move it before sitting down on the edge of the bed. I try to shift my thoughts to literally anything else when Sam jumps in front of me.

"Dad," he says, eyes wide. "What about the pool? Can we go?"

Benji lights up immediately. "Yeah! It's heated!"

Nash groans quietly beside me. "I was hoping they'd forget."

Sam turns to me with a pleading look. "Did you bring my swimsuit? Please tell me you did."

"No, bud. I didn't pack anything specifically for a night in the mountains. I thought we'd be home tonight," I say, and Sam visibly deflates, throwing his little body down on the bed with a dramatic sigh like I've just ruined his life. I hate disappointing him, but he can always go in his shorts. Before I can suggest it, though, Nash speaks.

"Hang on," he says, standing up and grabbing his bag.

"Benji's extra stuff is in here. I always throw in extra of just about everything in case he forgot to pack something."

Sam perks up in an instant at Nash's suggestion. "Wait, really?"

"Yeah," Nash says, already rummaging through a neatly rolled-up bundle of clothes while I'm silently praying that there's an extra set in there. Though I doubt Nash would've mentioned it if he wasn't sure. "Benji might be a little taller than you, but these should work for the pool."

Nash tosses him a folded bundle, which looks like swim trunks and a T-shirt. "Try that. If it fits, we're good."

Sam runs quickly to the bathroom to try it on, and I'm feeling inexplicably grateful for Nash at this moment. "You packed an extra swimsuit?"

"Between him and his sister, I've realized you can never be too prepared," he says easily.

He didn't pack that suit for Sam specifically, and yet, I can't help feeling this quiet wave of relief anyway because it's one less thing I have to worry about.

"Thanks," I say quietly.

Nash shrugs and gives me a look that says it's no big deal, but to Sam, it's everything. I stand, taking a few steps toward the bathroom door and knock. "Hey, Sam, don't forget to rinse off first, okay? You've been in ski gear all day."

His groan comes through the door, but he doesn't argue as I hear the shower turn on.

"You too, Benji," Nash says to his son who's riffling through the clean clothes on the bed.

"Fine," he huffs, and I laugh at how much he seems to resist showering too, just like Sam.

Nash stands and stretches, then turns to me. "Want to rinse off before we head down?"

"Yeah, I'd love to, as long as we can hold them off from running down there without us."

"All we can do is try," he says with a wink, and I damn near melt. There's something about the ease between us that makes it feel like we've known each other for years.

Sam and Benji each take all of two minutes in the shower, barely rinsing off before they're back out in the room, hair damp and towels clutched in their hands, clearly impatient. Nash motions for me to go next, so I grab my bag and head into the bathroom, shutting the door behind me.

The steam's already fogged the mirror, and the air smells faintly of citrus. I turn on the water, peel off my clothes, and step under the spray. It's hot enough to sting at first, but after a day of skiing in the cold, it feels incredible.

I pump the hotel's citrus-scented shampoo from one of the full-sized bottles mounted to the shower wall, working it through my hair slowly before rinsing it out. Then I grab the body wash and soap up quickly, knowing there are two boys out there bouncing off the walls waiting for the pool.

By the time my hand drags absently over my half-hard dick, I have to shut my eyes for a second and breathe. Now is not the time. Definitely not the time. But the thought of Nash coming in here next, stripping down and stepping under this same spray, does nothing to help my self-control.

I do my best to push the thought away and finish up as quickly as I can, shutting the water off so I'm forced to get out. I towel off, pull on the clean clothes I packed, and run a hand through my damp hair. I feel a hundred times better already.

When I step back out into the room, I glance over Sam and Benji to look right at Nash, and it feels like the air is knocked from my lungs. How can one person be so objectively attractive? It isn't fair. Shouldn't even be allowed.

He smiles at me, and before my brain catches up, my mouth betrays me.

"I'm all yours," I blurt.

Oh fuck. Fuck, fuckity, fuck.

"The bathroom, I mean! It's all yours. Not me. I'm not—" Oh god, I cut myself off. My face is on fire, cheeks burning with embarrassment. I might as well have announced I was just in there thinking about him while I was naked.

How can I be this embarrassing?

I'm all yours?

I'm all yours?!

What is wrong with me?

I'm a grown man, for crying out loud, and I've never been this tripped up before. I've handled harder conversations with doctors, teachers, lawyers, and mortgage lenders without breaking a sweat. Usually, I can fake confidence, even when I don't feel it—something I've picked up from being a single parent—but suddenly, it's like that skill has completely evaded me. Because I said *that.*

Apparently, one attractive guy who's kind and has a good smile is all it takes to destroy me.

"Cool, thanks," Nash says easily, like he's doing me a favor by pretending not to notice how much of an idiot I am. He's got the biggest grin on his face, though, as he grabs his clothes and ducks into the bathroom, shutting the door behind him.

I flop back onto the bed and exhale hard, dragging a hand over my face.

"Are you okay?" Sam asks, leaning over me.

"Fine, bud," I say, clearing my throat. "Just waiting."

He shrugs, already moving on, but my brain refuses to follow. I can't stop replaying Nash's amused expression. Almost like he was holding back a laugh and politely ignoring the fact that I clearly lost all social awareness... and possibly my mind.

Now, tonight, I have to share a bed with this man after I just said *that*.

Fantastic.

CHAPTER 4
Nash

I need to hurry up, but I can't stop smiling over what Caleb just said. It was adorable.

He's probably out there beating himself up for his slip of the tongue, and all that does is make me want to walk out there and tell him he doesn't need to be embarrassed, that I liked it, but it feels too soon. We haven't even known each other for twenty-four hours, and the last thing I want to do is scare him off. So I bite my tongue and focus on finishing my shower, even if my head isn't cooperating.

It's strange, being around someone I actually want to flirt with, and feeling like I'm doing a terrible job of it. Hell, maybe I was the problem on every date I've ever been on over the years. Maybe they wanted to teleport away from me too.

I still can't believe I invited him to sleep in our hotel room, but I just knew I needed more time with him. There's something about Caleb that makes me want to lean in instead of playing it safe. There's a curiosity there, and a pull I haven't felt in years. I don't think I'm imagining the way our conversations keep skimming the line of flirting—or so I think—and after that slipup, I have to think we're both aware of it.

I hurry through my shower, toweling off quickly before pulling on my dry clothes. My chest is buzzing as I grab the door handle. I have to get it together before I walk back out there. The last thing I want is for him to feel like I'm laughing at him, when really, I'm just… hoping he's feeling a fraction of what I am.

I take a deep breath before opening the door. Caleb is laying on the bed while the boys are looking through the desk drawers for whatever reason.

"Pool?" I ask.

"Yes!" Sam yells as he and Benji run toward the door and yank it open.

I grab my keycard and water before seeing Caleb's bottle sitting on the TV stand. I pick it up and give him a questioning look. He nods, and I hand it to him.

"Thank you," he says shyly before we both make our way out the door to bring the boys downstairs to the pool.

They're practically bouncing off the walls, already animated about doing cannonballs, who can hold their breath the longest, and whether the water will be warm or not. All I know is I'm glad they can entertain themselves, and I don't have to go in.

Caleb walks beside me quietly. When I turn to look at him, I have to remind myself not to stare, but the urge is there. His blond hair is still damp, and he smells like citrus from the shower, making me want to bury my face in his hair.

As soon as we get down to the pool, I pull out the keycard to swipe us in. The moment we step inside, warm, humid, chlorine-filled air immediately hits us. There are a few other kids already playing in the pool, but it's not crowded.

The boys don't care at all that there are other people in here. They waste no time kicking off their shoes and tossing their towels down on the nearest chairs before cannonballing into the deep end.

Caleb and I both chuckle as we smile and wave to the other parents and grab the boys' stuff to bring it over to where we're actually going to sit.

"Dad!" Benji yells. "You have to count for us! We're going to see how long we can hold our breath."

"Alright." I chuckle.

"Go!" Sam yells, and I start counting out loud to make sure they know I'm participating. Caleb is quietly laughing as we both watch them hold their breath underwater. "Thirty-one, thirty-two, thirty-three." I count before Sam pops up. "Thirty-four, thirty-five." Then Benji comes up, gasping for air.

"I got thirty-three, you got thirty-five," Sam updates Benji.

"Let's go again!" Benji exclaims, and they're right back under.

I can't help but smile as I think about how if I hadn't walked up to Caleb this morning, none of this would be happening. Benji would've spent the day mildly disappointed, skiing a few runs, and wishing someone else had come with us.

Instead, he's glowing, having the time of his life.

"I'm glad they get along so well, " Caleb says after a moment with a big smile on his face. "Benji's a good kid."

I glance over at him and smile back. "So is Sam."

He nods, then looks down before looking back out at the kids. "He doesn't usually warm up to people this fast. I think today has been good for him. He seems to really like Benji."

"Benji is very social, just like his sister, Emma. I'm sure he was dreading being stuck here with just me again tonight."

Caleb leans back in his chair and stretches his legs out in front of him. His shirt rides up just a little when he moves, revealing a sliver of skin, and I rake my teeth between my lips. It's been a long, long time since I've been with a man. All I can think of now is what his skin would feel like under my hands, what he'd sound like if I kissed down the length of his stomach, and what it would be like to have him beneath me, eyes glazed over and trusting me to take care of him.

"I doubt that," he says quietly, almost like he's saying it to himself.

Fuck, I'm in trouble.

CHAPTER 5
Caleb

By the time we make it back to the room, the boys are still little energizer bunnies wrapped in towels, dripping pool water on the carpet, recapping everything they just did.

"Quick rinse off," Nash instructs. "Then we'll go eat dinner."

The boys scramble, each grabbing their clothes and taking their turn in the bathroom. Somehow, Benji manages to drop one sock and a shirt in the ten steps he takes to get to the bathroom. Nash laughs as he bends down to grab them and hands them off to him, who yells a quick "thanks!" as he closes the door.

He's only in there for a few minutes before he comes out and Sam runs in.

Nash tugs on a hoodie and turns to me. "You good with the restaurant downstairs?"

"Perfect," I quickly agree, more than ready for a real meal and not just half-finished ski lodge chicken tenders.

He smiles at me softly, and there's just something about

Nash that makes the space around him feel less chaotic. Which, in a hotel room with two energetic kids, is nothing short of a miracle.

When Sam comes out of the bathroom, we head back downstairs. The restaurant has a warm, laid-back feel with a mix of booths and high-tops, and the smell of garlic and herbs makes my stomach growl.

"Hi there, four tonight?" the hostess asks us.

"Yep, thank you," Nash confirms.

It's such a normal thing, but I appreciate how he didn't pause or defer to me. Even on the rare occasion I go out with friends, it feels like I'm always the one asking, therefore, the one planning. Unless it's one of those forced parent hangouts with Sam's friends' parents, but I wouldn't call birthday parties and awkward playdates "fun."

I've carried every decision on my own for so long—what to make for dinner, when to call the dentist, how to handle every holiday, every meltdown, and every morning school rush. I didn't even realize how much I've wanted someone to step in and just handle it once in a while. At least, I didn't dare let myself imagine having it since dating as a single parent seemed like too much. Not that Nash is my partner or anything. But still.

The hostess leads us through the dining room, and we settle into a round table tucked near the back. Nash pulls out the chair next to mine, and knowing he wants to sit next to me makes me smile.

We all pick up our menus as the hostess walks away.

"I think I want a burger," Benji shares after looking at the menu for thirty seconds.

"Does it have bacon? If it has bacon on it, it's probably

good," Sam says, completely serious, and I glance up from my menu to make eye contact with Nash as we both try to hold back a laugh. Kids are so funny.

"I'm getting the one with onion rings on top," Benji decides. "I'm starving."

"That chicken tender fuel running out?" Nash jokes.

"Yeah." Benji shrugs. "That was hours ago, Dad."

"I'm starving too," Sam adds on, and it's a mystery how in sync these two are already.

Nash shakes his head at me, grinning. "We've created monsters."

"Hungry monsters," I agree.

I let out a small laugh and lean back in my chair. This whole thing feels surprisingly easy and comfortable.

"Hi, I'm Cassy. I'll be taking care of you tonight. Can I get you anything to drink besides water?" the waitress asks, setting a jug of water down on the table.

"Water is great," Nash tells her.

"That works for me, too. Thanks."

"I want the onion ring burger," Benji pipes up.

"Oh, are we ready to order?" Cassy asks.

Nash turns to look at me, and I give him a nod.

"Seems like it. Sam, do you want to go next?" he asks, and my heart swells.

"I'll do the bacon cheeseburger! Can I have fries?"

"Of course," Cassy says as she writes down the order.

Nash turns to me instead of Cassy. "Caleb?"

He's just being polite, I remind myself. But, seriously, if this sweet, thoughtful, ridiculously considerate man keeps doing stuff like this, I'm going to need someone to tie me down before I float away.

I've spent so many years making sure Sam goes first—and

he always will—but it's rare for anyone to pause long enough to also see me in the equation. Nash not only prioritized Sam, but he's prioritizing me, too.

I clear my throat. "Yeah, uh, I'll do the chicken sandwich, please." At least my voice sounds steady, I think.

"I'll do the steak, medium, with fries," Nash says, rounding out our orders.

"Great, I'll go put that in. It shouldn't be long," Cassy confirms, holding her hand out for the menus.

As soon as she's gone, the boys dive into a debate over whose burger will be better. Nash leans back in his chair, arm draped casually over the top of Benji's, and I glance over at him. My eyes land on the sliver of skin peeking out from beneath his shirt. There's the start of a happy trail that leads straight to… somewhere very happy. I lick my lips before my brain catches up, and I immediately look away.

Jesus, I need to get it together. This is not the place.

When I glance up, Nash is already looking at me, an amused smirk tugging at his mouth like he's waiting for me to say something.

Heat crawls up my neck as I fumble for words.

"They really hit it off," I blurt, because apparently we're just repeating conversations now.

Nash chuckles. "Yeah, Benji will make friends in line at the grocery store if you let him."

"I can imagine that." I laugh. "Sam's usually a little more reserved. Takes after me, I suppose. It's good to see him enjoying himself like this."

"Well, you're both easy to like," Nash says with a smile.

I smile back, feeling overwhelmed in the best way. I truly can't remember the last time I smiled this much in one day. It feels good, really good.

I glance at Sam, who's dramatically reenacting a cannon-ball for Benji using just his hands and facial expressions, and smile softly at him because he seems to be having just as much fun as I am.

"You're doing a good job, you know. With him," Nash says, pulling my attention back to him.

Compliments always hit me sideways, mostly because I feel like most of the time they're not genuine, but this one lands right in my gut because coming from Nash, I know it is. "I don't know what I'm doing half the time."

"Yeah, well," Nash says, "I don't think any of us do. But it's obvious you're doing your best, he's a great kid, and that's honestly all you can do."

I nod, swallowing past the lump in my throat. He said it as if it were obvious. Little does he know, I've spent years wondering if I'm doing enough. If I am enough. If I messed up Sam's life because it's ultimately my fault his mom left. I've tried my hardest to give Sam the best life possible, and for once, Nash makes me feel like I am.

He just… sees me. And damn if that doesn't undo me a little.

Before I can come up with a semi-normal response that won't embarrass me further, the waitress returns with a tray full of food. The boys perk up immediately, shuffling items on the table to make space as she lays down our plates.

"Whoa," Sam says, eyes wide as he grabs a fry from his plate as soon as Cassy sets it down. "So many fries, this is awesome."

"Make sure you eat your burger, too," I remind him before he eats only fries for dinner.

"I know, Dad," Sam huffs, and I shake my head before I

take a bit of my sandwich, trying to resist the urge to look at Nash.

Except he shifts in his seat and his leg brushes mine under the table. It's barely a tap, but he doesn't move it. If anything, he presses it further into mine.

My heart stutters, and suddenly, I forget how to chew. I'm ninety-nine percent sure he's doing this on purpose. Or maybe he isn't. Maybe I just imagined it because I want it to have been on purpose. But I'm not. We are touching. And now if I move my leg, will it seem like I'm pulling away? But if I leave it there, is that—what, flirting? Am I flirting?

Oh god.

I finally swallow and glance up at Nash. He's cutting into his steak, and he doesn't look fazed at all.

I, on the other hand, am deeply fazed. He's sent me into an emotional free fall from gently nudging my leg under the table with his because after this? We're going to go upstairs… to share a bed.

A freaking bed.

With one blanket.

And no clear boundary line.

I need to focus.

Focus on Sam.

On my food.

On literally anything other than the man across from me, who might've just flirted, or maybe he just shifted his leg without thinking. I don't know, but I know what I want it to be.

I shove another fry in my mouth and nod like I'm part of the conversation the boys are having about whether or not ketchup counts as a vegetable, though I'm pretty sure it's a fruit. It doesn't matter, though, because I can still feel the heat of Nash's leg against mine, and I'm too scared to open my mouth out of fear of what might come out.

I've already embarrassed myself enough for one day.

But even as I sit here, pretending to listen, one thought keeps circling my head: I don't know what's happening between Nash and me.

I just really, really don't want it to stop.

CHAPTER 6
Nash

The room's quiet.

The boys fell asleep as soon as their heads hit their pillows about ten minutes ago. Now, Caleb is in the bathroom, and I'm in bed—the bed we're sharing tonight—in my boxers and a T-shirt, scrolling through my phone.

I've caught him looking at me multiple times throughout the day, and he always gets shy when he realizes he's been caught. It's cute. But after I caught him shifting in his seat when my shirt rode up and he licked his lips, I wanted to test something. I pressed my leg to his under the table, and he didn't pull away or flinch.

I'm not entirely sure what that means yet, but I think it's safe to say he feels this thing between us too.

The bathroom door creaks open, and he makes his way toward the empty side of the bed. I glance up at him. He's wearing glasses now, and they somehow make him even more attractive.

He pulls back the covers, and the mattress dips slightly under his weight as he settles in.

It's been a long, long time since I've shared a bed with someone. After my divorce, I learned to sleep alone, and it quickly became my new normal. Now, Caleb is here, lying just a foot away from me in the stark silence, and every inch of me is aware of him.

I set my phone down and whisper, "The boys are out cold."

Caleb lets out a soft breath. "Yeah. I had a feeling Sam was going to crash after the day we've had."

"They wore themselves out today." I glance over at Caleb, finally letting myself take in the slope of his shoulder under his T-shirt, the curve of his mouth in the soft light from the lamp, and those rectangular-rimmed glasses. "So, glasses?"

His cheeks turn red as he blushes, and I love that sight. "Uh, yeah, I wear contacts during the day."

"I like them. They look good on you."

He turns toward me slightly, his cheeks still flushed red. "Thanks again... for letting us crash here."

"You don't have to keep thanking me," I assure him. "It wasn't even a question."

"Sorry, I just..." he trails off, hands fidgeting with the blanket as a distraction. "I don't know what to do with myself right now."

His voice is quiet, surely to not wake the boys, and he looks nervous.

"You don't have to do anything," I soothe. "We're just lying here."

"I know," he says quickly. "It's just that... it's been a long time since I've been this close to anyone. That sounds pathetic, but I haven't shared a bed in years."

I nod. "Neither have I. Unless you count the kids."

He's still fidgeting, fingers twitching against the edge of

the blanket. I want to reach over and still them—take his hand in mine. But I don't.

Even with the tension boiling between us.

"I used to be better at this," he admits after a pause.

"Better at what?" I ask softly.

"At not feeling so nervous around other people, I guess. Or feeling like I'm about to say the wrong thing. Or move the wrong way. Or ruin… whatever this is."

"You haven't ruined anything," I tell him, wanting to reassure him. "You couldn't."

He lets out a quiet breath and turns slightly more toward me. There's hesitation in the way his body hovers, unsure if he should lean in or roll away.

"I think I forgot what it feels like to be seen," he says, his voice a little unsteady. "Not just as a parent or a coworker or a problem-solver. Just… me. As my own person."

The honesty in that confession cuts deep. It's quiet and raw and so real it makes my chest ache.

"I see you. And I like what I see."

His breath catches, and I hope I didn't just reveal too much, but from what I've gathered from Caleb today, it's that he wants someone else to take the lead sometimes. And I want to do that for him.

"There's absolutely no pressure from me, but if you want to be closer—if it would feel good to you—I wouldn't mind that. At all. Actually, I'd really like it."

There's a moment of complete stillness that's loaded with indecision. But then, slowly, he shifts toward me; so tentatively, so cautiously, like he's working up the courage to take me up on my offer.

"Uh, do you mind setting my glasses on the table?" he asks.

"Not at all," I say, gesturing for him to hand them to me. When I lean over, I turn off the lamp on the table as well, then settle back into bed.

"Would it be weird...?" He gestures vaguely toward me.

"Not at all."

In this moment, he seems like he needs me to show him how okay I am with this. I shift onto my back, and reach for him, pulling him into me. He closes the last bit of space, curling into me as he tucks into my side. His head finds my shoulder as his hand lands softly on my chest, and I lay my free hand on top of his.

"This okay?" I murmur.

"Yeah," he whispers. "It's perfect."

I hold him a little tighter in response as we lie there together and our legs tangle.

His body is warm against mine, and I feel the tension ease out of his shoulders as he settles into me. I don't know every-thing about Caleb—hell, I hardly know *anything* about Caleb —but I know this means something to him. I can feel how careful he's being, and I want to make it easy for him to stay, to breathe, to feel safe in my arms.

I rest my chin lightly against his hair, breathing him in. It's underrated how good it feels to hold someone like this, with no pressure for intimacy or more. It's just comfort and connection, and it's enough.

While I definitely didn't expect today to turn out like it did, something in my chest tells me that maybe, just maybe, this is the beginning of something more.

And for the first time in a long time... I'm not scared to see where this goes, and I have no desire to teleport anywhere.

I'm exactly where I want to be.

CHAPTER 7
Caleb

I wake up slowly, warm and sleepy, and not in any rush to move. For a second, I forget where I am until I shift slightly and realize there's a big arm wrapped around me, holding me tight.

Nash.

I'm in bed with Nash.

He's curled up behind me, his chest against my back, with his hand resting low on my stomach under the blanket. Our legs are tangled with his knee tucked behind mine—we're full-on spooning, and I'm the little spoon.

My body tenses a little as last night comes back to hit me in full force. How I awkwardly gave myself a pep talk in the bathroom about how this would all be fine. I couldn't stop fidgeting because I was sure I'd do something else embarrassing or mess up what's growing between us somehow.

Nash made me feel comfortable, though. He has since the moment we met. And when he offered to hold me, there was nothing in the world I wanted more than to be wrapped up in someone who made me feel that safe.

And now, I'm half hard because of it.

It's been a long time since I woke up with an erection, and as much as I want things to escalate, now is so not the time. Instead, I focus on steadying my breathing so I don't risk waking him and losing this connection.

The feeling of him—a man—wrapped around me, making me feel small, allowing me to be tucked into him, feels right in all the ways I'd always hoped it would. There's a deeper sense of comfort being in his arms, and somehow it feels far more natural than anything ever did with my ex-wife.

Nash shifts slightly, and I brace myself for him to wake up and let me out of his grip. But if he does wake up, he doesn't move away. If anything, he tightens his arm around me, pulling me in closer, even nuzzling into my hair.

I exhale slowly, sinking deeper into his embrace, letting my body mold to his. The weight of his arm draped around me, the warmth of his chest against my back, makes me feel cared for. Safe. Maybe even adored.

No one's ever held me like this, and I like it more than I should admit.

The fact that we met yesterday hasn't evaded me, and yet nothing about this feels rushed.

I don't know what this means for us, if there even is the potential for an "us" or if I'm just reading into something I shouldn't be reading into at all.

But, for now, I embrace this for all it is, because if it is a one-night thing, I want to soak it in fully.

I MUST'VE FALLEN BACK ASLEEP because the next thing I know, I'm being shaken awake.

"Dad, I'm hungry," Sam cries, and reality smacks me in the face, It rips me from the peaceful, warm bubble I wanted to cocoon myself in earlier as panic takes over, because I'm in the room with my son... and Nash and I are still spooning. *Shit.*

"Mmmm, morning," Nash breathes into my neck, and goosebumps break out across my skin. He's not freaking out, or at least he doesn't seem to be, as he slowly rolls over and untangles our bodies. The loss of him is immediate, and I wish I could ask him for five more greedy minutes. Or, ideally, skip the mountain altogether to stay snuggled up in bed.

"Dad?"

Right, right. Sam. There's no way I'd ever be able to lie in bed all day with Nash. Not when we have kids—and mine just saw me cuddling with a man.

He knows there's no right or wrong way to love. I've always made sure of that. I've taught him that families don't all look the same, that what matters most is kindness, respect, and love. That people get to love who they love, and no one gets to decide what that looks like but them.

But I've never said anything about myself. Not because I was hiding some big truth. More like I wasn't sure what that truth even was. I've always been a little unsure about my sexuality, and the one time I did try to ask for more to explore my desires, it backfired... badly.

So I convinced myself that maybe if I just focused on being a good dad, the rest wouldn't matter.

But it does matter.

Because if I want Sam to grow up confident in who he is —whatever that looks like for him—I can't keep hiding parts of myself. Not when there's nothing to be ashamed of.

It's a conversation I'll have with Sam soon when I figure out what to say.

"Yeah, we'll get breakfast soon. Just let everyone get up and get ready," I say to Sam. "Can you grab my glasses for me, bud?"

His little legs run around the bed to grab the glasses off the table, and he hands them to me.

"Thanks."

Nash shifts with all the commotion and turns toward me. My insides suddenly feel all gooey just from looking at his disheveled brown hair and seeing his sleepy smile aimed right at me.

"How about we go get breakfast, then come back here to get our gear before heading to the mountain. That work?" he asks, making a plan. *Another point for Nash.*

"That works for me," I confirm.

His hand reaches over, under the blankets, and gives my thigh a squeeze—and of course, my dick immediately perks up.

I bite the inside of my cheek, trying to play it cool, but I can feel the heat crawling up my neck. I've always blushed too easily, and Nash definitely notices.

He lets out a quiet laugh. "I'll hop in the shower first," he says, already sitting up. Then, with a quick glance back at me, grinning, he adds, "Give you a few minutes to… regroup."

He disappears into the bathroom, and I run a hand over my face, still feeling the ghost of his fingers on my thigh. I use the few extra minutes to get my heart rate back to normal and talk my body down.

That is until Sam speaks.

"Dad, why were you and Benji's dad cuddling?"

My heart lurches for an entirely different reason now.

"Oh," I panic. "Uh…"

Sam tilts his head, waiting, and I have no idea what to say, so I go with the truth. Or some version of it.

"I just… wanted to," I say honestly, even if it sounds weird out loud. "Sometimes grown-ups cuddle when they feel close to someone. It's… like a comfort thing."

He nods, chewing on that for a second. "Like when I sleep with you after a nightmare?"

"Exactly like that," I say, relieved.

"I hate nightmares." He shudders at the thought. "Did you have a nightmare?"

"No," I admit.

"Then why did you cuddle?"

There's nothing like children to make you figure out answers you don't know and explain yourself.

"Well," I start, stalling for time I don't have. "Because the comfort felt nice. I think Benji's dad is great, and being close to him just felt good."

Sam squints at me. "But you're a grown-up," he says, confused.

"I am, but grown-ups need comfort too. We get scared. We get tired. We feel things and don't always know what to do with them, just like you."

He seems satisfied with that, for now. "Okay," he shrugs, turning back to Benji.

"My dad's the best!" Benji declares, and I chuckle at that.

"He sure is," I agree easily.

I let out a deep breath, then practically collapse into myself when I turn and see Nash standing there. I must've missed the sound of the bathroom door opening.

Add it to the ever-growing list of embarrassing things I keep doing around him. My face is hot, and my heart is still racing as I think about how long he's probably been there and how much he heard.

I quickly get up to grab my stuff and head toward the bathroom. Nash is smiling at me as I approach.

"We can talk about that later, or never," I whisper as I walk past him into the bathroom.

"Sure, sure." He laughs as I close the door behind me.

As soon as I'm inside, I lean over the sink and splash cold water on my face. Nash makes me feel good, nervous. I forgot what it feels like to have a crush on someone, even if that sounds so juvenile.

Being with a man is something I've desired for so long, and even though this feels too fast and too risky—especially with our kids involved already—it's also something I know I need to allow myself to explore.

I just hope he feels the same. He's given me every indication that he does.

By the time I come out, sweatpants and a hoodie on, contacts in, and teeth brushed, Nash is helping Benji zip up his coat, and Sam is fully dressed. Nash looks over at me and offers a soft smile. "Just finishing getting them ready so we can go grab breakfast whenever you're set."

My heart swells. He didn't have to help Sam get ready while I was in the bathroom, but he did, and now he wants to keep spending the day together. I had a moment of doubt that he'd act weird or pull away, especially since I keep embarrassing myself, but he isn't.

"There's a breakfast place right next door," he adds. "It had good reviews. Does that work?"

"That's perfect." I smile. "Thanks for looking it up."

"Of course." He smiles back. "Alright, Benji, put your hat on and we'll head out."

"You too, Sam," I echo.

When we get outside, it's not snowing like it was yesterday. It's a slow, steady stream of big, fluffy flakes. The roads are finally plowed—not that I'm in any rush to leave. I want to soak up as much time as possible with Nash.

At the restaurant, we all order our breakfast, and the boys get the exact same thing. Then we head back up to the room to pack and get our gear ready to head to the mountain.

"Let's go to Bonanza for the first run," Sam decides as he tugs on his ski boots.

"Oh, yeah! I want to do that too!" Benji piggybacks on.

I glance at Nash, who gives the boys a big, warm smile. "We can make that happen."

A chorus of "yes!" and "awesome!" follows.

Every part of me is thoroughly impressed with Nash, because this man—who I only met yesterday—is already fitting into our little world like he's always belonged. He and his son are slipping into place beside me and mine. The way he shows up for me and Sam is answering questions I've spent years avoiding.

CHAPTER 8

Nash

Just like yesterday, today is perfect.

Normally, it'd be because there's inches of fresh snow for us to ski on, but today, it's because I woke up spooning Caleb. I would've stayed under the covers with him all morning if I could have, but the kids wanted breakfast, so skiing with him again today feels like the next best thing.

The boys are ahead of us now, side by side on the two-person chairlift, their skis resting on the bar. We're a chair behind them, and for once, I'm grateful for the separation to spend some alone time with Caleb.

Something is building between us, and I need to know if I'm the only one feeling it. It's not just the way he let himself sink into me last night or how he didn't rush out of my arms this morning.

It's what I overheard this morning.

He told Sam I'm great, that being close to me felt good.

Even though I didn't hear the whole conversation, I can't stop thinking about how honest that part sounded. Maybe he's not as far behind me in these blooming feelings as I thought.

He feels like the one I've been waiting years to find, as insanely fast as that sounds.

The boys are waiting for us off to the side of the drop zone, and once we catch up, they waste no time heading down the run. We follow, carving down the mountain a little more carefully than our sons, who have no concept of gravity or fear. *Ah, to be young again.*

At the bottom, the boys want to go again, of course. After checking the time, we agree to a couple more runs and load back onto the lift.

As soon as we get situated on the lift this time, Caleb turns to me. "Last night," he starts quietly, "that wasn't... weird for you?"

"No," I answer quickly, hopefully leaving no room for doubt. "It wasn't."

He nods slowly, like he's thinking through his next words carefully. "Are you...?"

I don't say anything for a second, and when it's clear he isn't going to finish his question, I think about how I want to word my response. "I'm bi. I've gone on a few dates with men since my divorce, but none of them ever led anywhere. In college, I hooked up with a guy a few times, but that's it."

He nods again, giving me a shy smile as his cheeks heat.

"Well, okay, cool. Thanks for telling me."

"Of course." I pause, studying him, sensing there's more he wants to ask, but he's probably holding back after asking about my sexuality. I want to give him the space to ask, but also let him know I'm not hiding any parts of me, either. "I married my college girlfriend. We divorced four years ago, and I haven't seriously dated anyone since. I've met a few men, but... they weren't right. I've enjoyed it, but it's been hard to find something real."

Caleb's gaze drops to the safety bar in front of us, fingers tightening just slightly as he starts twisting his hands around it. I don't know how he's going to react to that, or if he's interested in me at all, but with the way I'm feeling already, I want to lay it out there.

After a moment, he opens his mouth, but he swallows the words. "Fuck," he breathes to himself before trying again. "I've never been with a man," he nearly whispers, but I hear him loud and clear.

I'm not sure if that means he's interested in men but hasn't been with one, or if this is some kind of bi-awakening for him. Either way, he seems to be bracing for something that feels like a mix of judgment, discomfort, and maybe even regret, but he doesn't need to brace with me.

I reach over and place my gloved hand over his, trying to offer him that same comfort he was explaining to Sam this morning.

"That's okay," I say gently, because it is. He looks up at me, light blue eyes dusted with hazel locking on mine, and gives me a small smile.

I don't want to push him, but I'm curious about what this could mean for us. We only have so much time left here, and I'd hate for us to leave the mountains without him knowing that I'd love to keep exploring this connection between us. If he's not into it, then I'll lick my wounds and move on, but I can't do that until I know.

"You don't have to say more if you're not ready. But I want you to know I'm here. I'd like to understand what it means for you, if you ever feel like talking about it. I'm not expecting anything, I just wanted you to know I see you," I add.

He surprises me by flipping his palm to meet mine, glove

against glove, and gives my hand a squeeze. I wish the layers weren't there so I could feel his skin against mine without anything between us. Even like this, though, I can feel the way he's reaching for comfort. Just like last night.

"I've known for a long time that I'm attracted to men," he says after a moment. "But I've never acted on it. Honestly, never even really said it out loud like this before to anyone. Growing up in Missouri, it didn't feel safe to even think about it. Then I got married, also to my college girlfriend, and we had Sam. After the divorce, I didn't know how to go back and figure myself out. I feel too old to screw around with a stranger, and I don't want to date just to date. Plus, it's hard to leave Sam when I don't have to. We don't have family nearby."

I nod, feeling something shift in my chest at the longing and loneliness I hear in his voice. It's clear that sharing that took a lot of courage, and I'm grateful he trusted me to tell me that already.

"You don't have to have everything figured out," I assure him. "You don't owe anyone a label or an explanation—me included—and you're definitely not too old. Besides, you never know who you're going to meet and when." I smile, giving his hand a reassuring squeeze.

Caleb looks at me then, and for the first time since we started this conversation, there's relief in his expression.

"Thanks. When you held me last night, I felt like I could breathe for the first time in a long time," he murmurs.

I pause for a moment, knowing how hard it is to admit something like that out loud, especially when you've spent your whole life pretending you didn't need it. Or worse, telling yourself you couldn't have it because you grew up in a place where admitting your desires made you a target, so conforming was survival.

"I felt that too," I agree. "I wished we could've stayed like that for even longer."

"I'm really glad we met," he says with so many emotions in his eyes, and my heart damn near explodes in my chest.

"Me too, and I'd definitely like to see you again after this weekend," I finally admit, laying it out there.

He grins at me, and his eyes light up. "I'd really like that."

We're almost to the drop zone now, so I give his hand one final squeeze and pull away as the chairlift moves closer, lifting the bar as we get ready to stand.

This run is quieter for Caleb and me, not the boys, though, who are still having a great time together. All I can focus on is what Caleb just shared with me. He sounded like he was scared to say it out loud, which I understand.

During the years Tess and I were married, I hardly ever brought up my sexuality, mainly because it was assumed for me. She knew I was bi, and it never bothered her, or we never would've gotten married in the first place. But once you're married, or in any long-term relationship, people make their assumptions.

After we divorced, I started correcting people when they assumed I was straight. Even though everyone who truly mattered in my life already knew, there are so many people I'm around daily who didn't. And I'm fully aware of just how much strength it takes to step outside the version of yourself that's always felt safest to exist in.

I'm proud of him for sharing what he did today, and I still want more.

I want to know what his days look like when no one's

watching. I want to know how he takes his coffee, what kind of music he listens to when he's alone in the car, and what he does for work. I want to hear the stories behind the photos on his fridge. I want to know if he hums while he's doing the dishes and his favorite takeout restaurant. I want to know what makes him laugh so hard that he has to cover his face, or if he snorts.

I want to know the version of him that only comes out when he's comfortable, when he's safe.

This doesn't feel like a crush or a moment or a fling. It feels like a beginning.

And I don't want to miss any part of it.

CHAPTER 9

Caleb

By the time we reach the base of the mountain at the end of the day, I'm wiped out. Sam and Benji could've probably kept going until the lifts stopped turning, but I've had more than enough today in the best way.

I glance over at Nash as he unclips his skis. His cheeks are red from the wind, his brown hair is messy and wavy from his helmet, and when he catches me looking, he smiles.

"Ready?" he asks.

I nod even though I'm not. I don't want this to end. No part of me wants to get in the car, drive down the mountain, and go back to a life where none of this exists. My life back home suddenly feels a lot emptier by comparison.

We spent today laughing and taking advantage of the time we had on the lifts to get to know each other better. Nash told me more about his daughter Emma and how she's only six, but she can keep up with Benji, which is wildly impressive. He shared that he's from California but moved to Denver for college and never left. I told him about my work designing homes, and he asked thoughtful questions like he actually cared. He explained what he does in tech, and while some of it went over my head, I liked hearing him talk and watching his face light up when he mentioned his kids or a project he was proud of.

And now, as I carry my skis to the car, I already feel it slipping through my fingers, despite Nash saying he wanted to continue exploring this.

It's impossible to ignore the voice in my head that fears once we go back to our real lives in Denver, the little bubble we've been in will burst. He'll decide that a thirty-four-year-old divorced single dad with full custody, who's probably bi, or maybe gay, but has never even been with a man, isn't worth it. That feels like a lot of baggage to willingly agree to, but I'm trying to hold onto hope because Nash has done nothing but surprise me so far.

When we reach our cars, which are parked side by side, all four of us begin going through the motions of peeling off layers, tossing jackets, boots, snow pants, and the rest of our gear into the trunks. But my hands are slower than usual. For the first time in my life, I wish skiing came with more layers and more gear. More things to put away. Just... more time.

While I milk it as long as I can, Nash looks at me expectantly, and I feel the gravitational pull toward him.

"I'm really glad we met," he says in a low voice that's just for me when I make it over to him. "This whole thing... it wasn't what I expected when I booked this weekend, but I wouldn't change any of it."

My throat tightens. "Yeah. Me either."

"Can I text you to make plans to do this again? Or meet up back in Denver?"

I swallow hard, that rush of hope hitting me hard because I want that. God, do I want that.

"Yes," I rush out. "I'd really like that."

"Me too." He smiles softly at me. "I've got your number, and you've got mine."

I nod, and before I can say anything else, he takes a step closer, stopping just inches from me. My eyes rake over his handsome face until they land on his, and the air grows impossibly thick between us. I swallow and lick my lips, trying not to show how fast my heart is racing. Is he about to kiss me? There's no way, right?

He leans forward, and I stop breathing. But instead of closing the distance between our mouths, he tilts his head, lips brushing my ear, and he whispers, "I really want to kiss you."

The words hit me square in the chest because I've never wanted to be kissed so badly. He pulls away, and I look at him, startled and aching and feeling very, very alive. I suck in a deep breath, trying to compose myself.

"I would've really liked that," I admit quietly, my voice rough around the edges. "But... you know."

We both glance toward the boys who aren't paying us any attention whatsoever. Still, it's not the time or place. But the wanting is there, and this feeling isn't going anywhere.

"Maybe next time," he says, licking his lips.

I nod, biting back the smile that's threatening to take over my face. "Yeah. Next time. I'm going to hold you to that."

"Good thing I'm great at keeping my promises," he says with a wink, and somehow, even in twenty-degree weather, I damn near melt right here in the parking lot.

"Dad, come onnn," Benji groans behind me, immediately echoed by Sam.

"Guess that's our sign," I say reluctantly.

"Guess so," Nash confirms, but neither of us walks away.

Instead, he opens his arms, and I don't even think before I'm in them. I press my cheek to his shoulder and breathe him in, willing my body to remember this moment and this feeling. Nash's arms are warm, strong, steady, and they feel like everything.

"I meant every word, Caleb," he murmurs near my ear. "I'll text you when we get home."

I nod into his shoulder before forcing myself to pull away from the greatest comfort and acceptance I've ever felt in my life.

"Dad, can we do this again next weekend?" Sam asks, and I turn to look at Nash, who smiles at me.

"Nash and I exchanged numbers, so we'll talk and see when you boys can meet up again. How does that sound?"

"Awesome!" Benji cheers, and Nash and I laugh with our eyes locked on each other.

"Okay, let's head out," I say, closing the trunk of my car. Just as I'm about to walk to the driver's seat, Nash rounds the corner again, pulling me into him in another tight embrace and kisses me on the cheek.

"I promise the real thing will be even better," he whispers before pulling back, leaving me there, breathless. He's flipping my entire world upside down with a few words and a completely innocent kiss.

I open my car door and drop into the driver's seat, sitting here for a moment, completely taken aback knowing this man is just as affected by me as I am by him. That this man wants to see me and spend time with me. My heart is still pounding from those whispered words and the brush of his lips on my skin as I grip the steering wheel. He didn't have to say any of that, but he did.

For the first time in years, I don't feel ashamed, or like I missed my chance, or messed something up.

And the old pain that's dug deep into my chest every time I think about why my marriage really ended starts to loosen… just enough to hope I can finally have everything I want.

CHAPTER 10

Nash

"Hi, princess! I missed you," I say, breaking into a grin as I jog toward Emma.

"Daddy!" she yells, bolting toward me from Tess's car, her little legs pumping as fast as they can go. The second she's close enough, I scoop her up and spin her around, earning a squeal that makes everything feel a little lighter. She clings to me, burying her face in my neck for a second. "I missed you too!"

I close my eyes and just hold her there. Seeing her always makes me so happy, but I can't help but feel like I left part of my heart in the mountains.

"How was your boys' weekend away?" Tess asks as I lower Emma back to the ground.

"It was awesome, Mom!" Benji cuts in. "We met Caleb and Sam, and Sam's so cool. We skied together all weekend! I want to hang out with him again, it was so fun."

I laugh at his enthusiasm, but it also tugs at my heart because I haven't stopped thinking about Caleb for a second since we left. It's surreal how someone can take up so much space in my mind after such a short time, and I keep wondering if he's thinking about me too.

Now that I've had a glimpse of what dating could be like with someone who feels like they fit with me, I want to know what it looks like when we're not wrapped in a snowy mountain weekend, but in the chaos of day-to-day life with our children. Because the way he made me feel in less than forty-eight hours of knowing him? I'd be a fool not to chase that. Especially since it was the most fun I've had in a long time with someone—and the easiest.

Tess, Emma, and Benji are still catching up, so I pull my phone out to text Caleb, as promised.

> Made it back safe. Hope you and Sam did too.

He replies almost instantly.

CALEB:

> We did. Thanks for such a great weekend, Nash.

I can't help the grin that spreads across my face just seeing his name on my phone.

"Alright, kids, go inside. It's freezing out here," Tess says. "I'll see you next weekend. I love you!"

"Okay! Love you!" the kids yell as they bolt toward the house. She lingers behind, arms crossed, eyes narrowing just slightly as she looks at me.

"I've known you too long not to recognize that smile," she says with a knowing smile and teasing tone. "So... Caleb and Sam, huh? Who are they?"

Tess and I have always been friendly like this, even after the divorce. It was never dramatic or messy. She's a great person, just not the right person for me. Somewhere along the way, we both realized we made better co-parents than partners, and when we talked about separating and neither of us fell apart, we knew it was the right call. She's dated since then, and I can tell she's genuinely happier now. And despite everything, we've stayed on the same page where it counts: The kids always come first. We even live a couple of streets apart on purpose to make it even easier for them and us.

"They're a father and son we met skiing," I say, trying to keep my voice neutral, even though my heart hasn't figured out how to slow down since we left them. "Benji and Sam hit it off right away. Caleb and I just... connected."

"Connected," she repeats, amused. "That's your word?"

I give a little shrug, but the truth is, it was more than a connection. It felt like a collision in the best way. Completely inevitable and impossible to ignore.

"Well, Benji seems pretty thrilled," she says, nodding toward the house. "Think you'll see them again?"

"I hope so," I admit, and I don't even try to hide the smile this time.

She studies me for a second, then grins. "Good. It's nice to see you... I don't know, happy."

"Thanks, Tess."

She takes a few steps back toward her car, then glances over her shoulder. "Alright, have fun with the kids. I'll see you on Sunday for drop off."

"See ya," I call after her.

She drives off, and I stand here for a second, gathering myself before heading inside.

Benji and Emma are already digging through the snack cabinet, and all I can do is smile.

"I'll make dinner soon," I tell them. "Just let me unpack a bit, okay?"

"Okay," they both say in unison, which makes me happy since they aren't demanding food right this minute.

It only takes me about twenty minutes to unpack all our gear and get our clothes in the wash before I start dinner. I settle for spaghetti and meatballs, and the kids have no complaints. After dinner, I get them cleaned up and ready for bed, and when the house finally quiets down, I grab my phone and open my texts with Caleb.

> Would you rather stay in a stranger's hotel room or drive home in a snowstorm?

I stare at the screen for a second, heart thudding, as I wait for the three little dots to appear.

CALEB:

> That's a tough one. Though I did just have a great experience staying in a stranger's hotel room, so I think I'd have to go with that. As long as it's the same stranger.

Another smile takes over my face at his response.

> What a lucky stranger

CALEB:

> He even let me sleep on my favorite side of the bed.

> Sounds like a perfect match

CALEB:

> I think you're right about that

> That stranger's kind of hoping he doesn't stay a stranger much longer.

Three dots appear, then disappear, and reappear. Finally after what feels like an eternity, he texts back.

CALEB:

> Yeah. Me too.

CHAPTER 11
Caleb

I t's been two days since we got back, and I still can't stop thinking about Nash. We've been texting as much as we can, and I feel like a teenager, which is both ridiculous and a complete rush.

Yesterday morning, he sent me a selfie of him helping Benji and Emma put on their snow gear. They were bundled up in their snow pants and coats, and I must've stared at it for a solid five minutes. It felt like he was sharing a glimpse into their lives.

When they were finished, Nash sent another photo of a lopsided snowman with a carrot nose, scarf, stick arms, and what looked like pinecones for eyes. It made me laugh, but it also made me ache a little. It felt like I was watching something just out of reach, something Sam and I didn't quite fit in with yet, even though that wasn't his intention.

A small part of me is terrified by how quickly these feelings are staking their claim. A week ago, I wouldn't even let myself think about dating again. And now, all I want is more time with him. To have plans for when we'll see each other again. To play in the snow with Sam, Nash, Benji, and Emma. To wake up with his arms around me. I can't think of anything I want more, honestly.

Sam shifts his feet on my lap, drawing my attention back to the Christmas movie we have on. Every night in December, we watch a different holiday movie. It's our own little tradition. This month has always been our favorite, and now it feels like it has the potential to be even more special for a whole new reason.

The rational part of me knows I should attempt to pump the brakes because I'm feeling too much, too fast. But I can't seem to help it. Not when every part of this feels good in a way I forgot was possible.

I pick up my phone, rereading our texts from earlier. He said he had a couple of meetings this afternoon, but I want to restart our conversation.

He's a director at a tech company, which somehow makes him even more attractive because, of course, he's a leader. He's thoughtful and intentional and all the things I'm very into.

I start typing: Hope your meetings went well.

Then delete it because that's boring.

> Kind of wish we were back on that mountain right now.

My finger hovers over it, then I hit send, and he replies less than a minute later.

NASH:

> Same. Especially if I got to wake up with you pressed against me again.

I bite my lip, try not to grin at my phone, and make sure

the screen is tilted away from Sam as I try not to overthink my response.

> I'd like that, a lot

NASH:

> I keep thinking about that weekend like I dreamed it, but I don't think I could make up a guy like you

My heart feels funny, and it's impossible to hold back my smile now.

> I've been thinking about you too. Probably way more than makes sense for 48 hours

NASH:

> Can I call you tonight?

> Yes, I'll let you know when Sam goes to sleep.

It's been years since I've looked forward to hearing someone's voice at the end of the day. We haven't talked on the phone yet, but knowing he wants to makes my heart race with anticipation.

As soon as the movie is over and Sam is tucked into bed, I head to my room, shutting the door behind me. I quickly brush my teeth and strip down to my boxer briefs, then pull out my phone to text Nash.

> Sam's asleep.

My nerves are at an all-time high. Even though we spent the weekend together and have been texting since, this feels different. There's no buffer of a screen or distraction of the kids, just the two of us to fill the silence that hopefully isn't awkward.

As soon as my phone buzzes, I answer it on the first ring. *Oops, definitely not playing it cool.*

"Hey," I say, already smiling as I hold it up to my ear.

"Hey," he says back. His voice is as warm as I remember. "How was your day?"

I laugh softly. "Better now that we're talking."

"Yeah?" There's a smile in his voice. "Same here."

I reach over to turn the lamp off and put the call on speaker phone before scooting down my bed to get comfortable against the pillows.

"This is the opposite of playing it cool, so forgive me, but... I didn't expect to miss you this much so soon," I confess. And weirdly, it's easy. Easier than I ever would've thought possible. It's the kind of admission I would've swallowed down before meeting him because it would've made me feel exposed, and my own vulnerability has been used against me in the past.

But with Nash, it feels right.

I don't care if it makes me seem needy. He cracked something open in me, and there's no stuffing it back inside now. It's strange how fast a connection can form with some people, and he's that person for me. I want him to know I'm not here to play games, and if he doesn't want someone like that, I'd rather know now than become any more invested.

"Me either," Nash says. "I keep thinking about our night together and how I wish we had longer together."

I let out a shaky breath, soaking in the comfort of knowing he's seemingly just as affected as I am.

"I didn't want it to end," I tell him, honestly.

"It doesn't have to," he reassures me, and I smile.

There's a rustle on the other end of the line. I picture Nash getting more comfortable, settling into his bed, and wish I were there.

"You said your week was busy?" I ask, wanting to find a time to see him.

"Yeah," he says on an exhale. "Work's been a mess, and Benji keeps asking when we're gonna see you two again."

My heart jumps. "So does Sam. He keeps asking if we can go skiing with you both again this weekend."

"They're kind of a perfect match," Nash says, and I can hear the affection in his voice.

He's not wrong, and I can only hope there's a hidden meaning in that statement about us being a perfect match, too.

"I keep wishing we somehow lived next to each other, instead of twenty minutes apart," I murmur, eyes fixed on the ceiling. "Like… right next door, ideally."

"I'd probably be at your house right now," he says without hesitation. "You'd open the door, let me in, and I'd finally kiss you."

My fingers tighten around the phone that's resting on the pillow beside me. I imagine opening the door and him wasting no time as he steps up to me, grabs my face, and slams his mouth to mine. A quiet gasp escapes me before I can stop it.

"I want that," I whisper, my voice barely there. "So much."

"I think about it constantly," he admits. "Think about *you* constantly."

Heat pools in my stomach, my body already reacting to the sound of his voice and the images he's painting with it.

"You did say you're good at keeping your promises," I tease, my voice rough with want.

"Oh, I am," he assures me, and I can hear the smile in his voice—smug, seductive, and sincere all at once. "And that one's at the top of my list."

"Fuck," I gasp. My dick is thickening in my boxer briefs, and I want to stroke myself to the sound of his voice, to the fantasy he's building. It's unbelievable how much he's affecting me even through the phone. I swallow and decide to take a chance. "What would you do... once you were inside?"

His exhale is slow and sounds a lot like a *mmm* sound. "You sure you want me to tell you that?"

"Yes," I beg. "Tell me."

There's a moment of silence, and the anticipation only makes me harder. I squeeze myself through my briefs, thumb brushing over my tip before the urge to free myself becomes too much. I lift my hips and get naked, hand wrapping around my cock just as I hear his voice.

"I'd close the door behind me." He continues the fantasy. "And I'd press you up against it so you could feel what you do to me. I'd grip your hips, kiss you slow at first, then deeper like I've been thinking about since that night in the hotel."

A gasp leaves my lips. I need lube. He's only talked about kissing me, but the image of it is filthy. I bite my bottom lip, reaching into my bedside drawer for lube, struggling to stay quiet even though no one's around to hear.

"Then what?" I ask, desperate now, holding my dick in my grip while I find the bottle.

He hums low in his throat. "Then I'd take my time with you. Grind against you, kiss you until you're so worked up you're begging me to take you to bed." He pauses, and it's filled with tension through the phone. "Would you let me undress you, Caleb?"

I nod even though he can't see it. "Yes."

"I'd bring you to your bedroom," he continues. "Let my hands get acquainted with your sexy body. Touch every inch of you until you're shaking for me, desperate for more."

A low sound escapes my throat despite my best efforts to swallow it down.

"That's it, I want to hear you," Nash encourages.

I squirt some lube into my hand and start stroking my cock. My entire body is keyed up with the kind of tension that won't go away on its own. I want him—the weight of him, the heat, the pressure of his body against mine. Need to feel it.

"I'd pull your shirt off first," he murmurs, "then push you back onto the bed and climb over you, grind down on your clothed erection until you're writhing and begging for me to get us both naked. I want to see how you look when you fall apart under me."

"Fuck," I breathe.

"That's what I want, Cay," he confirms. "Because you're in my head. Every second of every day, I think about you. I keep wondering how it's possible that I've only known you a few days and I already want you this much."

The confession floors me—more than anything else he's said—even though my mind is spinning on his nickname for me.

"I want you too," I whisper. "So fucking badly."

There's another pause as I continue to stroke myself to the fantasy he's building in my head.

"You touching yourself right now?" he asks, voice low and knowing.

My breath stutters. "Yes."

"Let me hear what I do to you."

It's the permission I didn't realize I was waiting for. I let out a breathy moan that I can't hold back.

"Fuck," Nash groans. "That's the sound I've been dying to hear."

"I've been hard since you said you'd kiss me," I admit. "I can't stop thinking about you pressing me against the door... kissing me like you own me."

"I would. You'd feel it in every kiss. Every time I touched you, you'd know who you belonged to in that moment. What else do you want? My mouth? My cock? My ass?"

My hips thrust into my fist, and I let out a loud moan. He's asking me what I want, and I don't want to hold back. "Your cock in me. Want you to fuck me."

It's Nash's turn to let out a groan on the other end of the line.

"Mmm, yes. I want to be on top of you," Nash continues, breath ragged. "Want to watch your face when I sink into your tight hole. I bet you look so fucking pretty when you come. So fucking sexy when you fall apart."

My hand speeds up, his voice in my ear spurring me on.

"I'd go slow at first," he says, "stretch you with my fingers, get you nice and ready for my cock. Would you like that?"

"Yes, oh fuck yes," I pant, getting close.

"Good, because then I'd ruin you like I promised. I'd hold you down while I fuck you until you can't think of anything else but me for days. Can't feel anything else but me."

"Nash," I gasp his name, barely able to get it out. "You're gonna make me—"

"Do it," he commands. "Come for me. Don't hold back, I want to hear it."

My orgasm crashes through me, and out of pure habit, I bite down my groan, trying to keep it quiet but not entirely succeeding. My hand slows as I ride it out, body trembling with how much I needed that release.

On the other end of the line, Nash groans softly, like the sound of me unraveling is enough to undo him, too.

There's a moment of quiet, both of us catching our breath.

"You still with me?" he finally asks, voice hoarse but tender.

"Barely." I laugh, still breathless. "Jesus, Nash. That was... that was incredible. You're incredible."

"You are too, Cay. I wish I was there."

"God, me too," I say honestly.

"Go get cleaned up for me since I'm not there to take care of you," he instructs, and being told what to do by him is almost enough to make me hard again.

"Okay." I shuffle to get up, bringing the phone with me to the bathroom, wetting a washcloth, and cleaning my stomach where I came on myself.

"Alright, I'm heading back to my bed now."

"Good," he murmurs. "And Caleb? I know I said this, but I really do want to spend more time with you."

I swallow hard, warmth blooming low in my stomach again, but for a different reason this time.

"I do too."

"Good," he says, and I can hear the smile in his voice. "When can we plan something?"

"Well, I have Sam every night since I don't share custody," I start, knowing that'll immediately make it harder for us to plan anything, but hoping that's something Nash will be okay with. "He has a sitter for nights I have something, though. I could see when they're available. What's your schedule like?"

"That's okay, we'll make it work. We can also hang out with the kids, of course," he says easily. "I'd just really like to get my hands on you alone sometime soon, too." There's a low chuckle in his voice that sends a shiver down my spine. "My ex and I do alternating weeks. So, I have my kids till Sunday night. If needed, she'd probably take them for a night if I gave her a heads up. We try to stick to the schedule, but we're both pretty flexible and help each other out."

I smile into the phone, oddly comforted by how relaxed he's being about all of this. "That must be nice."

"It is. Co-parenting's a hell of a lot easier when you still get along with the other person."

"Yeah," I say softly. "That part sounds great."

"What about you and Sam's mom?" he asks, and I knew we'd have to talk about her eventually.

I shift on the bed, pulling the blanket over my legs even though I'm already warm. "She moved out of state. We were already barely holding things together before she left. She calls sometimes, and Sam talks to her on holidays or his birthday when she does, but... I'm pretty much it. My parents are still in Missouri, and her parents no longer talk to me either after the divorce."

There's a pause, and I don't mean for the words to come out so heavy, but they are. They always are when I admit how much of this I carry on my own. But Nash doesn't rush to fill the silence. He just lets it sit there for a second before saying, "That must be a lot."

"Yeah."

"I admire the hell out of you for it," Nash acknowledges,

and hearing those words from him makes my throat tight with emotion.

"Thanks. I don't hear that much."

"Well, get used to it. I want you to know how incredible you are."

I breathe out a quiet laugh that's filled with relief and gratitude, all tangled together.

"I've never…" I trail off, the words catching at the vulnerability of saying this out loud, but I do anyway, because I want to be honest with him. "I've never really had that with anyone. Someone to support me, I mean."

"That breaks my heart, Cay," he says. "How about lunch tomorrow? It's not romantic, but we can go when the kids are at school… If you have time, of course."

"I'm in. I'll check my calendar in the morning, but I'm in."

"Good," he says. I can hear the grin in his voice. "I'll make it the best lunch you've ever had."

I laugh softly. "That's a bold promise."

"I meant what I said; I keep my promises."

And I believe him.

We chat more about how our days went, and when we finally hang up, it's much later than I meant to stay up. But I don't regret a second of it.

CHAPTER 12
Nash

I got to the restaurant ten minutes early because I couldn't keep half-assing work I didn't care about knowing I'd see Caleb today. After checking the time approximately a thousand times this morning, I decided to just leave the house and come to the restaurant Caleb and I had agreed to have lunch at.

It's kind of ridiculous that I'm behaving this way. I'm thirty-six. I've been married, divorced, and attempted to date a handful of people over the years. I've tried the whole swipe right, small talk "so what do you do?" dance, but nothing has made my heart feel this uneven, hopeful, beating-out-of-my-chest feeling I'm experiencing right now knowing that Caleb will be here soon.

I'm even more excited after our phone call last night.

I don't usually have phone sex, but I could hear in his voice how worked up he was and how much he desired that guidance to get him there.

Now all I want is to hear those grunts and moans in person, to see the look on his face as he falls apart for me.

Caleb's given off bottom energy since day one, and lucky for us both, I don't mind taking the lead.

The waitress comes back to drop off two waters at the table I'm waiting at, and as soon as she walks away, Caleb opens the door and strides in.

He's wearing a navy coat, that's different from his ski jacket, and a gray beanie. His cheeks are flushed pink from the cold, and he's scanning the tables until his eyes lock on mine. He smiles and makes his way toward me, tugging off his beanie and running a hand through his hair. His smile softens a little as he gets closer, almost like he's trying to tamp down his excitement, but that just won't do.

Without wanting to wait another second, I stand and meet him, pulling him into a hug before he can say anything. He sinks into it immediately, arms wrapping around me like he needs this just as much as I do.

"Hey," he whispers against my shoulder.

"Hey," I murmur back, holding on a second longer than I probably should in a public place.

When we finally pull apart, he gives me a quick, flustered smile before we walk back to the table and slide into the booth on opposite sides.

"You look good," I compliment.

"So do you," he replies, eyes flicking to my mouth, and I want to kiss him right then and there, but I know the middle of a Mediterranean restaurant isn't the best place for me to kiss him for the very first time.

He shrugs off his coat and runs a hand through his hair again like he's trying to shake off nerves.

"I missed you, Cay," I say. "Even caught myself rereading our texts like a dumbass this morning."

That earns me a full grin. "Yeah? I was doing the same thing."

"Thanks for making this work." I lean back, trying to relax. "I really wanted to see you."

"Didn't take much convincing," he says easily. "I wanted to see you too. Work can wait."

"It definitely can."

His eyes drop to the menu in front of him, and I force myself to look too even though I already know I'm not going to remember anything I read.

"You good with splitting a couple of things?" I ask instead. "I don't want to waste time trying to figure out what to order."

"Yeah," he says with a smile. "As long as I get to keep sitting across from you, I'm good."

"You always this smooth?" I ask, raising an eyebrow.

He tilts his head, like he's actually considering it. "No," he says with a self-deprecating laugh. "Definitely not."

"You're not making it easy to take this slow," I murmur, eyes flicking back to him.

Caleb blushes, and I can tell he's trying not to look away, so I reach for him with my leg under the table and wrap my ankle around his.

"I like it when you do that," he says quietly.

"Yeah?"

"Yeah," he confirms.

We order and continue to talk. Our food arrives faster than expected, but we barely touch it. We talk a little about work. He tells me about a massive house he's designing for a client, and his job seems infinitely cooler than mine. Then he asks, "So, what does Christmas look like for you guys this year?"

"Depends," I say honestly. "Sometimes Tess and I will do

parts of Christmas together since we do get along, other years she takes them for Christmas Eve, and I get Christmas morning, or vice versa. This year is still up in the air."

Caleb nods slowly. "So, you're not sure yet?"

"Not completely." I pause. "Why? What do you and Sam have planned?"

He shrugs, a little sheepish. "We usually do the same thing every year, and it's usually just us. Which is fine, but—" He cuts himself off, like he's not sure if he's saying too much.

"But?" I prompt, wanting to know what he'll say.

"It just gets a little lonely sometimes," he admits. "I've had a lot of good holidays with Sam, of course, and I love him to pieces. But sometimes I wish I had someone. I feel guilty for saying that because it should be enough, but I can't help but want to wake up with a house full of good chaos. It feels like he deserves more, too, than waking up, opening his gifts in ten minutes flat, then sitting there alone while I cook for just us. Everyone else seems to be surrounded by love and family, and I just sometimes wish we had more of that."

The weight of his words hit me. I reach across the table to take his hand in mine. I want to tell him we should have our own Christmas together, but I don't want to make any promises I'm not one hundred percent sure I can keep.

"That sounds hard," I say instead. "Even if it's good in its own way. The years that the kids are with their mom, I feel the weight of that loneliness too."

Caleb lets out a breath, eyes on the table. "Yeah. I always feel bad because we have everything we need, and still, I can't help but want more."

"Maybe this year will be different," I say, hoping that I can figure out a way to make his Christmas better. "And you're not selfish for wanting more. We're human, and we crave connection. You should never feel guilty or bad for that."

"Thanks, Nash." He gives me a small smile as I squeeze his hand.

After we finish and pay, I walk him to his car, hands shoved deep in my coat pockets as the cold winter air bites at our exposed skin. I want to kiss him, plan to kiss him, as long as he's okay with it. He told me he's never been with a man before, and the last thing I want is to make him uncomfortable.

When we get to his car, neither of us reach for the handle. We just stand there, close enough to feel the warmth radiating off each other in the crisp December air.

Caleb turns to me, eyes lifting, then dropping briefly to my mouth, and the tension between us is palpable.

"I keep thinking about you kissing me," he murmurs, and that kicks my heart rate up.

I feel like I'm sixteen again about to have my first kiss. Except I'm not sixteen, and this isn't just some silly crush.

"I still want to. Will you let me? Out here in the open?"

He swallows, taking a moment to steady himself, then nods his head just slightly. "Okay."

I step forward, cupping his jaw with my hand, thumb brushing lightly against his cheek. His skin is cold from the air, just like my hand. He tilts his face toward me, breath visible in the winter air.

"I've wanted to do this all day," I murmur.

He licks his lips as his eyes drop to my mouth, and I lean in slowly, giving him another second to back away. But he doesn't, and when our lips finally meet, it's like a silent explosion between us.

The kiss starts slow, but when I feel the sharp exhale he

lets out against my mouth, I deepen it, letting my tongue tangle with his. The peppermint from the mint he just had after lunch is thick on his breath. Caleb's a bit more reserved, but he isn't pulling away, and I think I know what he wants. I tilt his head back, fully taking the lead, and his whole body relaxes and coils tighter at the same time. The air between us shifts from tentative to electric the more I guide him. His body presses into mine, and I feel the heat of him through the layers. I groan into his mouth and he swallows the sound.

It's hot to the point I barely remember we're standing in the bitter cold, and then I remember other people exist.

It takes every ounce of strength I have to break apart from him, but we are in public, and I don't want anyone to say anything that might make him want to hide away. He's panting, and I lean my forehead against his, still craving that connection.

"Holy shit," he whispers, feeling his warm breath against my cheek.

I smile, pulling back just enough to look at him. "Worth the wait?"

His eyes are darker now, cheeks flushed from more than the cold. "Yeah," he breathes. "Yeah, it was."

"Good," I murmur, brushing my knuckles down the side of his jaw. "I can't wait till next time."

His mouth twitches, that perfect blend of nerves and need. "Next time," he echoes.

"I'll text you when I get home," I tell him, leaning in for another quick kiss before reluctantly letting him go. He climbs into his car with a dazed sort of grin on his face as I stand here and watch him drive away, already craving the next time I get to kiss him again.

CHAPTER 13
Caleb

The first kiss I've ever had with a man is also the best kiss I've ever had, and I don't know what that means.

No, that's a lie.

I do know what it means.

It means I was right—that my sexuality isn't something I can keep ignoring. Kissing Nash felt right in a way no other kiss has. Not even to my ex. The feeling of his lips on mine, of him taking control, of him being the assertive one, made me feel like for thirty-four years I was living in black and white, and he just flipped the world into color.

My hands are tight around the steering wheel, and I keep replaying it on a loop in my mind. And I don't know what to do with myself. I'm a grown man with a kid and responsibilities and routines. I rebuilt our lives after the last one cracked in half—and somehow this thing with Nash is already feeling like my future.

I want more.

So much more.

More in a way I've never craved anything in my life.

I'm ready to let go of the fears, the hesitations, and the what-ifs that usually keep me stuck in place, because there's something about Nash that makes all those worries vanish.

It's probably because he's the exact opposite of my ex-wife in every way.

He's kind, caring, open, and supportive. And even though I still barely know him, there's something in my soul that calls to him.

With Nash, nothing feels forced or performative. I don't have to over explain or shrink myself or pretend to be someone I'm not. I don't have to play it cool—not that I've done a good job at that, anyway.

It's terrifying how much I already trust those feelings, trust him.

I pull into my driveway and see his name on my phone already.

NASH:

Made it home to finish my work day. Still thinking about that kiss, by the way.

I smile so big it takes over my face, which is becoming an everyday occurrence now. As soon as I get into my living room and drop down onto the couch, I type out my reply.

Same, I want to do it again.

He replies instantly.

NASH:

That can be arranged.

Thank god I also primarily work from home, because if I

had to be in an office right now, there'd be no way I could act normal around my coworkers.

> Wish we could've blown off work.

His reply is immediate.

NASH:

I'm not above using sick days for personal fun.

I smile, shaking my head, heart beating faster as I try to flirt back.

> You're distracting, you know that? Ever since we met, you're all I think about and then you went and kissed me like that. There's no way I'll be able to focus on anything other than you.

The typing dots appear. Then stop. Then appear again, and I hold my breath until his message lights up my screen.

NASH:

I've never wanted to take someone on a real date and drag them back to bed so badly at the same time.

> You don't have to choose.

NASH:

Fuckkkk, Cay. We need more time together. Today wasn't enough. It only made me want you more.

I look at the time and realize I have an hour or so before

Sam gets home from school. The desire pulsing through me right now is growing deeper.

I set my phone down on the coffee table, letting those words and that lingering kiss course through me. The way his hands guided my jaw, the way his tongue slid between my lips, the grunt he made. He has the quiet confidence of someone who knows what they want... and it's me.

Fuck, I'm horny again because of him.

My hand grips my already hard dick, giving it a tentative stroke—and that's when I realize I don't have any lube down here, because I've never had the urge to jerk off in my living room before, but Nash has me all messed up in the best way.

Without thinking, I shove my pants all the way off, hop off the couch, and run to the kitchen. My dick is free and swinging, and in this moment, all I can do is laugh at how ridiculous I've been acting lately. I feel like I'm young again —naked, turned on, and running around the house trying to find something to use for lube as I skid barefoot across the cold tile floor.

It's stupid and impulsive, and if someone saw me through the window, I'd probably never recover. But there's a thrill in it, and it feels so goddamn freeing and liberating to give into everything I want. All the things I wasn't able to enjoy or explore as a teen out of fear, or until recently, really. I'm finally giving myself permission to rewrite the parts of me that used to flinch at my own desires and allow myself to want Nash, a man. To think of his lips. His body. His smile. His kindness. To think of how good it felt to be kissed by him out in the open. How seen and wanted and desired he makes me feel.

My eyes land on the bottle of olive oil on the counter, and I grab it. I jog back to the couch, heart pounding. I'm painfully hard at this point, but the second I settle back into the cushions and wrap my oil-slicked hand around myself, the silliness and seriousness I found myself in falls away.

I close my eyes and picture Nash. His hands and the way they'd feel on my skin, dragging down my chest, holding me right where he wants me. I imagine his body pressing down on mine while I'm underneath him, exactly like he described on our call last night. His voice low, telling me how he'd take me apart.

My breath catches in my throat as I stroke myself slowly and let thoughts of him take over completely. I want to let him wreck me. I want to fall apart for him, with him. I want him to stretch my hole and fill me up with his cock.

Nash doesn't know it yet, but being full from my fingers or toys is my favorite way to come. Even if I've never had a real dick inside me before, I've been imagining it for far too long, and now, I'm imagining *his* cock replacing my dildo and making me lose my breath as he fills my hole. I want to ride him, to show him how good I can be for him. I want him to split me open and feel him for days, want to show him how much of a slut I can be for his cock.

I bite down on a quiet moan and let my hips move, losing myself in the fantasy, in everything I want and haven't imagined being a real possibility until now. My heart's pounding at this visual in my head, and I'm so close already.

I feel like I'm unraveling and coming alive at the same time thinking about his happy trail I saw at the hotel restaurant, thinking about how big his hands felt on my jaw and wrapped around my body, the feeling of his cock pressed against my ass when we woke up together.

Fuck. I need more of him.

My strokes get faster; my fist gets tighter. I can feel my orgasm building, and I don't want to hold it back.

My body shudders, chest rising and falling fast, and it's his name on my lips as my orgasm hits me. "Nash," I moan, back arching as I come all over myself with a gasp.

For the first time in a long time, or maybe ever, I don't feel weird or embarrassed afterward like I do when I jerk off to porn. I don't rush to clean myself up or carry around shame.

I just feel… alive.

CHAPTER 14

Nash

A ll I've thought about since lunch with Caleb yesterday —besides how much more I want to kiss him, touch him, press him up against something solid and hear the sounds he makes when he comes—is what he said about Christmas.

I keep picturing Caleb and Sam waking up to a quiet house on Christmas morning. No second set of hands sneaking down to fill stockings. Just Caleb, alone in the living room the night before, wrapping last-minute gifts under the glow of string lights, setting out cookies even though he knows he'll be the one to eat them.

In the morning, he'll make coffee while Sam tears into his presents. No one to sit beside him on the couch with sleepy eyes and bedhead. No one to say "I'll handle breakfast" or to throw a dish towel over their shoulder and help clean up the mess. Just him, doing it all quietly, holding it together with a smile for Sam's sake, but no arms to fall into once the excitement fades and the silence creeps back in.

I don't want that for him. I want to give him something

different. Let him feel what it's like to be taken care of for once.

Which means, if I want all of that, we need to introduce Emma and Sam.

My phone is already in my hand, and I hit the call button before I can overthink it. It rings twice before he picks up.

"Hey," Caleb says, sounding pleasantly surprised by my random call.

"Hey, I had an idea I wanted to run by you."

"Okay," he says slowly. "What kind of idea?"

"Are you and Sam free this weekend?" I check.

"Yeah, I think so."

"I was thinking maybe we should go back up to the mountains. We could do a day trip, or if you'd like to do overnight, I can find a place for us. Emma and Benji would come too, and we can see how they all get along once Emma's in the mix."

"I'd love that," he says happily. "Sam would too."

I smile, already pulling up the vacation rental site on my laptop.

"Good. I want to see you again, Cay."

"Me too," he murmurs. And I can hear the smile in his voice.

"I'll text you the details once I find a place," I say. "And... I'd really love to wake up wrapped around you again, but I'd also like to do more."

"You have no idea how much I want that," he says, letting out a soft laugh.

"Mmm, don't distract me now." I laugh. "I'll text you soon. Bye, Cay," I say before hanging up.

I click through cabin after cabin, but it doesn't take long to find the perfect one. It has two bedrooms—one with bunk beds for the kids and one with a queen bed for us. The floor plan shows the rooms on opposite sides of the cabin, split by a cozy living room and a small kitchen. It's perfect.

I send him the link with a quick message.

> Think this one has our names on it.

His response comes fast.

CALEB:

> Looks great to me. Can't wait!

There's only one more thing I need to do before booking it. While I'm not required to tell Tess what I'm doing with the kids, we always give each other a quick heads-up when we're taking the kids somewhere overnight. I pull up her contact and hit the call button.

"Hey," she says, picking up on the second ring. "Everything okay?"

"Yeah," I confirm. "I wanted to let you know, I'm planning to take Emma and Benji up to the mountains again this weekend. Just found a cabin for Saturday night."

She hums knowingly. "And does this cabin happen to include a father and son duo I've heard about recently?"

I laugh, not even trying to hide it. "Yeah, it does."

"Well, as long as you send me the address, I think it sounds great."

"You're the best."

"I know." She pauses. "And hey, I'm happy for you, Nash, really."

I glance over at the rental listing still glowing on my laptop screen, and a warmth settles in my chest. "Thanks," I say. "Me too."

As soon as I set the phone down, I book the cabin and the confirmation email pings in my inbox. I take a screenshot of it and send it to Caleb with the address.

This cabin should have plenty of space for all of us—and just the right amount of privacy for the things I'm aching to explore with Caleb.

I'm mildly worried about how fast we're moving—especially since we're involving the kids, but two of them were there when we met, and for all they know, we're simply planning the trip the boys have been asking for. Besides, I don't plan to tell them anything until we allow ourselves to fully explore our feelings.

Besides, I have a damn good sense of who I am at this point and what I want, and it's him. I'm not willing to risk missing out on this once-in-a-lifetime feeling, especially when he seems so all in too.

"Dad?" Emma's voice calls from down the hall. "Benji just spilled his cereal all over the counter."

I sigh, already standing, and shaking my head.

"Coming," I call back.

I'll always be a dad first, but for the first time in a long time... I've got something good waiting for me too.

CHAPTER 15
Caleb

"Hey, bud," I say, looking in the rearview mirror at Sam. "Remember Benji's sister Emma will be there this weekend too. So let's make sure everyone's included, okay?"

He groans. "But, Dad, she's little. She probably won't want to race." He pouts.

"She's six, which is only a couple of years younger than you. Not that little, according to you when you were that age," I remind him, parking the car in the lot Nash and I agreed to meet in. "And I'm guessing she can keep up if she's anything like her brother."

"Fine," Sam says, already unbuckling his seatbelt and reaching for the door handle before I've even turned the engine off.

A couple minutes later, Nash's SUV pulls in a few spots down from where we parked, and the second I see him, my nerves pick up. If this were anyone else catching feelings this fast, I'd probably roll my eyes and say there's no way you can fall for someone that hard that fast. But here I am, fully invested after one weekend in the mountains, a mutual phone jerk off conversation, and a lunch date.

The second the car's parked, Benji hops out of the car, and Nash opens the door behind him to get Emma. She's a little smaller, bundled like a marshmallow in a purple coat with braids poking out from under her hat. She waves at us, and I melt a little on sight at how cute she is.

"Sam!" Benji yells, running over to us.

"Hi, Sam!" she echoes from next to her dad.

Sam glances at me, then waves back. "Hi."

Nash and Emma walk over to us. "Don't worry, little man. She's tiny but fierce," he says to Sam who smiles at him.

When Nash reaches me, he pulls me into a hug. His arms wrap around me tightly, and I sink into him as my cheek brushes his maroon jacket.

"I wish I could kiss you right now," he murmurs into my ear, and same.

I pull back slightly to look at him, and his bright blue eyes meet mine. I swallow, suddenly aware of how close our faces still are. "Me too," I say quietly. "Later."

He nods, squeezing my arm once before letting go. "I promise."

Even though we're spending the weekend together with our kids, I don't want to kiss Nash in front of Sam. Especially without talking to him about it first. Once we know more about what this is, then I'll have that conversation with him. But for right now, all he needs to know is that we're here to spend another weekend with our new friends.

Sam's mom walked out when he was three, and even now, years later, there are days when he asks why she didn't want to stay. I've spent every day since trying to make him feel safe and secure again. The last thing he needs is to get attached to someone who might not stick.

Even if I desperately want Nash to stick.

Even if I have a gut feeling Nash will stick.

That's why it makes sense for us to do something "for the kids" because as much as I want to chase this feeling, I won't let it cost Sam his sense of safety. Not unless I know—for sure—that it's going to last.

We focus on getting the kids dressed and ready, then ourselves, and once everyone is bundled with their boots on and skis and poles in hand, we head toward the lifts. Emma sticks close to Benji and Sam, who are already planning what they want to do today, and it seems like the three of them will get along just fine.

The five of us head to the six-person chairlift, and it scoops us up. The snow from last weekend isn't coating the trees anymore. It's a blue sky, sunny day, and the snowcapped mountains that surround us are stunning as usual.

At the summit, the kids take off first—Benji leading, Sam right behind him, and Emma following like a tiny purple rocket. Nash and I trail, just like last weekend, and as I suspected, Emma is able to keep up with the boys.

"Wow, she's amazing," I call out to Nash.

He grins, watching her carve her way down with the boys. "She's a show-off," he says with pride. "But yeah, she's pretty great. She can definitely hold her own when we're out here with Benji."

"I'm impressed, honestly." Because for six, she's really confident.

"She started when she was three. We were a bit nervous to start her that young, but since Benji was skiing, she wanted to be just like her brother. I spent a lot of time working with her those first two years. She picked it up pretty quickly. I think having Benji made her want to be better faster because he always complained about not wanting to wait."

I can't help but laugh as I shake my head at that. "Kids."

"She might be younger than him, but they both challenge each other endlessly," he says.

I smile, watching them zip along ahead of us, bundled up and fearless.

BY THE TIME we finish skiing for the day, I'm wiped out. My body is aching, and I'm dreaming of hot chocolate by the fireplace before being wrapped up by Nash in bed.

I'm following behind Nash as we drive down the windy, snowy roads toward our cabin. It's only about ten minutes or so before Nash turns into a driveway. We approach a log cabin with a window wall and a large wraparound porch with Edison lights strung up. It's beautiful and so very Colorado.

Nash parks, and I pull in right beside him. He helps Emma out of the car before heading up the stairs to unlock the door. Emma and Benji are grabbing their backpacks from the trunk, and Sam does the same, eager to get inside with them. As soon as Nash opens the door, the kids barrel inside, and he walks back to his SUV. I only have a duffle bag, so I grab that and walk over to see if Nash needs help with anything.

"Anything I can do?" I ask, coming up next to him as he's shuffling through the trunk.

I see his eyes flick to the house and then back to me. "You can give me a kiss while the kids are out of sight."

"Mmm, I can do that," I say as I step closer to him. He pulls me in with his right arm and gives me a kiss. It's not a peck, but it's not a full-on earth-shattering makeout session either. Regardless, I can feel the passion behind it, and it only makes me look forward to tonight even more.

"Can you grab that grocery bag right there?" he requests when we pull apart, pointing to a reusable shopping bag.

"Sure thing."

"Great, that should be all we need," he confirms, pressing the button to shut the trunk before picking up the cooler and carrying it up the front steps as our boots crunch over the packed snow.

Inside, the cabin smells faintly of pine and wood smoke. It's small but thoughtfully laid out—as the floor plans showed—with an open kitchen, stone fireplace, and a long table in the dining room. They've also put up a Christmas tree with red, white, and green bulbs and white lights. It feels like the perfect touch to make this stay even more special.

As expected, the boys are already in the room with the bunks, and I bring our bags to the other room. It looks just like the photos with a white duvet and patterned pillows. I set my duffle and his backpack by the closet door in the room and make my way back to the kitchen to help Nash.

"Dad, did you bring my crayons?" Emma asks her dad as I round the corner of the kitchen.

"Sure did, check your backpack, I stuck them in there for you."

"Yay!" she yells, hurrying to get them. A moment later, she has her coloring book open and starts filling in what looks like a penguin on ice skates.

Nash continues to unpack the cooler, and I rush over to help him with the bag I've set on the counter.

"Thank you again for planning all of this. It's already been an incredible weekend," I say as I pull out a head of garlic, a bundle of fresh rosemary, and a tiny bottle of olive oil from the bag he set on the counter.

"I needed more time with you, and another night with you even more," he whispers.

"Oh yeah?" I raise an eyebrow, trying to sound playful, but inside I'm jittery with nerves in the best way. The anticipation of his hands on me tonight has goosebumps breaking out across my skin.

He flashes me a look that's somehow both innocent and loaded, and we're both well aware Emma is still at the kitchen table coloring, even if she is absorbed in her own world. "Yeah. But first, we cook."

"Okay, let me get the fire started first to really set the vibe," I say, already crossing the room toward the fireplace to take a moment to breathe. I grab some of the kindling they left out and place a couple of small pieces of wood on top. The kindling catches fast, and soon, with the addition of bigger pieces of wood, the flames catch and are crackling behind me. I turn on the TV and click over to YouTube, searching for my favorite Christmas playlist.

"Are you a Christmas music guy or is this gonna drive you nuts in ten minutes?" I ask as I hover over a holiday classics playlist.

Nash shoots me a grin from where he's chopping herbs at the counter. "Depends. If you start playing a country Christmas playlist, I'm walking out."

I snort. "Okay, that's fair."

"I like the old stuff, though," he adds, tilting his head toward the music I have queued up already. "This kind of thing is my favorite."

That's all the confirmation I need as I hit play.

"My mom used to put this kind of music on while she

wrapped presents. She always said Bing Crosby made everything feel more festive."

Nash hums. "That's a nice memory. Even if it wasn't all snowy, white Christmases."

"Yeah," I say softly. There's a thread of curiosity in his voice I don't miss, probably wondering what Christmas looked like for me growing up and my life in Missouri after the little I shared last week. "So, how can I help? And what are you making?" I redirect the conversation as I step up next to him.

"Roasted garlic chicken and mashed potatoes," he says, mincing fresh garlic.

"Do you always cook like this on ski weekends?" I ask, reaching for a knife so I can help chop.

"Only when I'm trying to impress someone," he says without missing a beat.

"Oh, so this is your A game?" I bump my elbow into his side. "All for me?"

"And Sam, can't forget him."

"I could never."

He leans in slightly, eyes still on the cutting board. "Don't knock it. We'll see how well it works on you tonight." He winks. Then he brings his mouth right next to my ear as he whispers, "I bet it'll have you *begging* for more, Cay."

A full-body shiver runs through me at the low rasp of his voice, and I have to set the knife down before I accidentally cut myself. I take a deep, steadying breath, and when I turn to look at him, he's already gone back to chopping.

This man.

CHAPTER 16

Nash

Dinner is great, but it really does taste even better because of who I'm sharing it with.

Caleb asks Emma questions about school and her favorite books, and she lights up like a little star, talking and talking while the boys inhale their food. Sam barely pauses to breathe between bites, and when Benji asks for seconds—mostly of the mashed potatoes—Caleb grins at me from across the table.

As chaotic as my life can feel with two kids, two schedules, and never enough hands, the feeling of adding Sam to the mix should make it more complicated. But instead, with Caleb here, it feels like maybe it'd be easier.

We just fit.

It's the exact thing I was scared I'd never find. I've spent so long assuming I'd have to bend someone into my life, make space they didn't really want to fill on weeks my kids were with me, compromise until the connection felt more like work than ease, all because they didn't understand my responsibilities as a co-parent or my friendship with Tess.

But tonight doesn't feel like fitting him into anything.

Doesn't feel like squeezing him into the gaps. It feels like adding on to make room for something—or two someone's—who were always meant to be here.

Just like I had a feeling it would.

"Alright, who's ready to watch a movie?" I ask, and the three kids push away from the table, chairs scraping back as they all shout, "Me!"

"Do you want me to make popcorn?" Caleb asks, glancing at me as he collects a few dishes from the table.

"That sounds like a great idea."

He smiles at that and turns toward the kitchen while the kids rush into the living room, claiming their spots on the gray sectional. Emma burrows into the corner with a snowflake blanket wrapped around her shoulders while Sam and Benji argue over which movie to watch.

"Come on, let's watch *Home Alone*," Sam says.

"But *Elf* is way funnier," Benji counters.

"I want to watch *The Santa Clause*," Emma pipes up.

"Hey, guys," I say, interrupting their conversation. "Why don't you see what this TV even has on first?"

"Oh yeah," Benji says, reaching for the remote.

I head back into the kitchen to help Caleb finish up. The smell of melted butter is in the air, and it makes the cozy cabin feel even cozier with the sound of the kernels popping in the microwave.

I find two big bowls in one of the cabinets and set them on the counter to pour the popcorn into.

"The kids are debating what Christmas movie to watch, so I have to know, what's your all-time favorite?"

"That's a hard question." Caleb huffs a laugh. "Umm, probably *Elf*."

"That's what Benji wanted, too." I smile. It's so simple,

but it feels like more proof that we mesh so well together. "We'll see what they landed on."

"What's yours?" he asks.

"I think I have to go with *National Lampoon's Christmas Vacation*. Though, I don't think that'll be on the voting board tonight," I say with a laugh.

"Probably not, but you and I can watch that another night. I love that movie too." Caleb smiles, and I nod, grabbing the popcorn from the microwave and pouring it into the bowls. We each grab one and walk into the living room to find *The Grinch* queued up on the TV.

"Alright, I like this one. Good pick, team," I say to the three of them who are all under blankets waiting for us.

After handing a bowl to Benji, I turn off the overhead lights, leaving only the warm glow from the tree and the flicker of the fire. On-screen, the movie starts, and the kids are under their blankets, crunching popcorn, and giggling through mouthfuls.

Caleb leans into my side, and I don't fight the urge to rest my hand on his thigh under the blanket we're sharing.

The movie plays on in the background, but I've stopped paying attention. All I can focus on is Caleb being so close to me. I need more connection, to feel even closer, so I reach for his hand, sliding my fingers through his. He gives me a small squeeze when our fingers interlock, and my thumb grazes over his skin. That's all it takes for the noise in the room to fade.

How can he already feel like everything to me?

How can I already miss him when he's right in front of me?

It doesn't make sense. But at the same time, it makes more sense than anything else has in a long time.

When the movie ends, Benji and Sam run to the bunk room, and I carry Emma since she fell asleep.

"I can get them to bed if you want to stay out here all snuggled up," I say to Caleb as I hold Emma in my arms.

"You sure?"

"Yeah, you look cozy. I'll be right back."

In the room, Benji and Sam are already changing into their pajamas.

"Don't forget to brush your teeth," I remind them, and as expected, I'm met with groans.

"And Sam, don't forget to say goodnight to your dad, he's still in the living room."

"Okay." He nods.

They do what they need to do, and when Sam runs into the living room, I watch Caleb give him a hug and tell him he loves him before Sam runs back to the room. He and Benji claim the top two bunks, leaving the bottom one for Emma. One by one, I say goodnight, flip off the lights, and close the door behind me.

The second I step back into the glow of the living room and see Caleb waiting for me on the couch, something quiet and certain settles in my chest. The fire is still glowing, and the couch looks even cozier now with the blanket rumpled. I drop down next to him and pull him into me.

"You tired?" I ask, kissing his cheek.

"Nope," he says with a smile.

"Good, there's a lot I want to do with you that doesn't involve sleeping." I smirk. "Bed?"

"Yeah. Let's go." He nods, his cheeks blushing red.

I grab his hand and tug him off the couch, leading him down the hall with an urgency I can't hide. The bedroom door clicks shut behind us, and I turn to face him. Without a word,

I reach for him, one hand gripping his hip as I pull him in until there's no space left between us.

The second our bodies connect, his breath stutters, and it makes me ache in the best way knowing I have this effect on him. I slide my hand up his spine until my fingers are teasing the strands of his dirty blond hair. He leans in, closing the last few inches between us, and when our mouths meet, everything else fades.

The kiss starts soft, but there's too much anticipation for it to stay that way. Caleb's hand slides to the back of my neck, fingers tightening like he needs me closer. I open for him without hesitation, and when his tongue finds mine, it sends a full-body shiver down my spine.

I press him back until he's pinned to the wall, my body glued to his, just like I told him I'd do to him on our phone call. I roll my hips into his, chasing the friction, and he groans into my mouth. It's the hottest thing I've ever heard.

It's messy, sexy, and electric.

I pull him off the wall and walk him back toward the bed, not breaking contact, not wanting to lose a second of this. We fall onto the mattress together, tongues still tangled, and I straddle him. I move against him, grinding down on his erection I feel through his sweatpants as he gasps into my mouth.

I kiss the corner of his mouth, his jaw, down his neck, before tugging his shirt up and off, pausing just long enough to look at him as he lays beneath me. His chest is solid and lightly defined with a faint trail of blond hair that leads down from his chest. I can't help but follow it with my eyes, stopping at his waistband, to where I'm sitting on top of him.

"You're so fucking beautiful," I murmur, raking my eyes back up his body.

He stares up at me like I just knocked the wind out of him. There's so much awe and hunger in his eyes. I want to praise and devour him.

"Is this okay?" I check in with him.

He nods. "Yeah."

My hands skim along the light dusting of hair on his chest once again before I lean forward to kiss along his pecks, licking and sucking one nipple in my mouth before moving to focus on the other.

His hips lift up beneath me, and my eyes flick to his to see him biting his bottom lip. He looks like he's holding back, afraid to say what he wants, so I give him room to show me. I grind against him a little harder, and his head tips back against the pillow, a low moan breaking free from his throat.

Finally.

"Tell me what feels good," I whisper, brushing my mouth along his jaw. "Or just keep making noises like that, and I think I can figure it out."

His laugh is breathless. "I don't really know what to ask for."

"That's okay." I kiss the corner of his mouth. "Just let me take care of you. But if you don't like anything, tell me."

His fingers curl into my shoulders, holding on.

"Yeah," he agrees. "Okay."

I start to move against him again, grinding our bodies together. The friction is almost too much through our sweat-pants, but also nowhere near enough. I guide his hips up to meet mine the best I can, and that's when I hear the hitch in his breath, the soft "fuck" whispered.

We keep moving together, grinding and dry humping, until we're both panting.

"Jesus," he breathes. "Nash—"

I slow down, giving him a second. "You okay?"

He nods quickly. "So okay."

His smile pulls at my chest, and I lean forward to kiss him again.

"Do you want more?" I ask when we break apart, wanting to taste him. It's been well over a decade since I've touched a man like this—since college. And yet with Caleb hard right in front of me, I'm certain I've never wanted anything more in my life.

He told me he's never been with a man before, and I want to show him how good it can be, even if my own experience is limited.

He bites his lip and nods at my question. I waste no time pushing up to my knees and move from atop of him to strip him bare. I'm rewarded with the most beautiful sight.

He's hard, flushed, and leaking with trimmed hairs at the base of his slightly left-leaning cock that's already wet with precum at the tip. His thighs tense slightly as my hands slowly trail up his skin. He's so beautiful.

"Still okay?" I ask quietly.

He nods once again. "Yeah. Just… nervous. But in a good way."

I lean forward, ignoring his erection right now, pressing a kiss to his stomach, then another on his left hip. His breath hitches as I move slightly until my mouth is hovering just above his tip, and I look up at him.

"Yes," he says to my silent question. "Please."

I give him a tentative lick before closing my mouth around his head, letting him adjust to the sensation, and listening for every sound he makes as I take him deeper.

He exhales sharply, one hand fisting in the blanket beneath him, the other reaching out like he's unsure where to put it. I reach up and take it, threading our fingers together and resting them on his hip as I take his shaft down my throat a little farther, also adjusting to the feeling. His hips twitch up instinctively, and I focus on relaxing my throat so he can take everything he wants from me.

"Fuck," he whispers, voice catching. "That feels so good."

I hum around him, and he moans in response.

His hand squeezes mine as he moves it to the bed, his hips bucking in the air. I pull off him to regain my breath, and tease his shaft, licking up and down. When I take him back in my mouth, I look up at him, and his lips are parted, eyes dark and glassy, chest rising fast.

"Oh, fuck, Nash," he finally grits out.

I take him back into my mouth and keep going, because I want to see what it looks like when he falls apart for me. As much as I want to keep his hand in mine, I want to make him come more. I undo my hand from his, curling one around the base of his cock, and bring the other one to his balls. His stomach flexes, and he lets out a choked sound, hips twitching like he's barely holding himself back.

His reaction tells me he likes his balls played with, so I move my mouth to suck his balls while stroking him with my hand.

"Jesus," he gasps, voice hoarse. "You're gonna—fuck— Nash, I'm not gonna last."

"That's the point, baby," I say after I pop off of him. "I want your cum."

His balls are tight now, so I lick a stripe under them, and he whimpers in response. I make a mental note of that and do it once more before dragging my tongue back up to swirl around his swollen tip. I take his cock back in my mouth, hollowing my cheeks and setting a pace that makes his thighs tremble. He moans—louder now—and he's tensing like he's trying to keep control.

But I don't want him controlled.

I want to undo him.

"Nash," he whimpers. "Nash, I'm… so close."

That's all I need to hear to keep my mouth wrapped around him, and it's only a second before I taste the first pulse of his cum on my tongue. He comes with a choked cry, and I suck him through it, not wanting to pull away until he's completely spent.

"Holy shit," he breathes after a moment, and I can't help but chuckle at his response as I pull off his dick.

"You taste so fucking good, my god," I praise.

He turns his head, looking at me with a mix of awe and something deeper. "I really want to return the favor," he says, a little shy, "but I'm nervous. I've never done this before."

"I can finish myse—"

"No," he cuts off. "Sorry, I want to. I really want to. Will you guide me? Tell me what to do?"

I smile, loving that he wants me to take the lead. "Of course I can, Cay."

Moving up the bed, I strip my pants off, and my hard dick springs out. As hot as telling him to drop to his knees would be, I'm not going to ask him to do that the first time he puts my cock in his mouth, especially because I laid on the bed. Learning his limits is far more important, but the fact that he's eager for me to take the lead is a big plus.

"Crawl between my legs," I start, and he moves quickly,

looking up at me with such eagerness in his eyes. "Get your tongue nice and wet, and lick me from the base to the tip."

"Fuck," he whines so softly before doing exactly what I say. My erection swings slightly as he finishes the swipe of his tongue.

"How did my cock feel on your tongue?" I ask.

"I really liked it. Fuck, I'm already getting hard again, and I don't even know how that's possible." He laughs, but his cheeks burn up at the admission.

"Hey." I lean forward and reach down, propping his chin up with my fingers. "I don't want you to feel shy or embarrassed around me ever, you hear me? You want something? Tell me. You like something? Tell me. You don't like something. Tell me. I want to know everything about you, baby."

His throat bobs and his breath hitches.

"Okay. Keep telling me what to do, it's really hot."

I smirk at him, knowing that when we get more comfortable with each other, we'll be able to have a whole lot of fun.

"Put the tip in your mouth and taste me with your tongue, see how that feels."

He does just that, wrapping his lips around my cock, and goddamn, is that a sight to see. He looks so good with his lips stretched around me, looking up at me with desperate eyes that are pleading for direction and praise.

"So good, baby. Give me a suck... Yes, just like that," I praise as he does what I tell him. "Now, try to take me deeper, suck my shaft, lick m—"

I cut myself off because, oh my god, he's going for it, and it feels incredible. His wet mouth wraps snugly around me, his hand joining at the base as he twists his wrist where he can't fit yet. If this first attempt is any indication, I've got no doubt he'll be able to deep-throat me soon.

"Jesus. You suck my cock so good."

His face breaks out in a smile, as well as he can around me, and he moves with more intensity.

He's not holding back at all. He's mimicking my movements, palming my balls, swirling his tongue around the tip, licking and sucking with so much enthusiasm. It feels like he's been waiting his whole life for this experience.

"So good, Cay."

He bobs his head up and down, gagging a little as he tries to go deeper.

"How do you take more?" he asks me, so innocently, even as he wipes the spit from his mouth with the back of his free hand.

"With practice, you'll learn how to breathe through your nose and relax your throat more, but you're already doing so well," I praise. "I'm already so close."

His mouth quickly moves back to join his hand that hasn't stopped stroking me. He flicks his tongue, swallows, and when he looks up at me and makes eye contact, I'm done for.

"Gonna... come," I tell him, trying to give him enough time. "Pull off," I manage to get out.

He pops off my dick, then leans over while he's still stroking me, mouth open and tongue out. The sight pushes me over the edge as I come all over his lips and tongue. A few pulses land on his throat and cheek.

"Holy fucking shit," I breathe out. "Holy fucking shit, baby. I can't believe you just did that. That was so hot."

"I've always wanted to try that." He smiles as he licks his lips and swallows my cum, cheeks burning red at his admission, and I am scrambling to pull him into me.

I wrap my arms around him and lick my cum off his cheeks and throat as he laughs and squirms in my arms.

There's so much joy in the room. For a split second I worry we'll wake the kids with how playful we're being.

"Nash!" he squeals, and I laugh. Keeping him in my arms, I kiss him all over—his cheeks, his lips, his neck, his forehead —because I'm in complete awe of him in this moment. "You're so amazing."

He pulls back slightly. "Was that okay? Too much?" he asks. Once again, it's shy, and I sense a hint of self-doubt over what he just did.

"No, you were perfect. How was it for you? Was it everything you hoped it would be?"

His cheeks somehow grow redder and he nods. "It was amazing. I've fantasized about that so much. I... I've always thought I'd enjoy giving head, but with you, it was so much better than anything I imagined."

I groan at that. "How are you real?" I ask, because I truly don't get it. He's perfect for me. "Your mouth felt so good. I want to explore all your fantasies with you."

He gulps, looking down, and I reach out to tip his chin up.

"Hey, I mean that. Anything you want, I want to give you."

He nods. "Thank you. I just... I'm trying to wrap my head around being able to finally let myself have what I've wanted for so long."

"I'll give you anything you want. Anything."

He nods against me, and we lie there in the quiet for a few minutes, our bodies tangled together, until I push up.

"Alright, let's clean up before bed. We've got kids who could barge in at any time."

He groans, and it's adorable, but he lets me help him up. As soon as he's upright, I kiss him before walking over to the door to make sure the coast is clear. I tug him down the hall toward the one shared bathroom in the cabin, and I forgot how much fun sneaking around trying not to get caught is… except it'd be my kids catching their parent.

Thankfully, we make it into the bathroom without being seen, and I turn on the water, waiting for it to get hot. As soon as it's the right temperature, I turn to Caleb. "After you, baby."

CHAPTER 17
Caleb

Nash keeps calling me baby, and it's making me melt.

I don't care if it's a common pet name. It's what *he* calls *me* now, and I want to be his baby.

For the first time in what feels like forever, I don't feel embarrassed or ashamed for wanting to be wanted like this. At least, I'm trying really hard to keep those emotions at bay because I'm happy. Really happy.

The water is the perfect temperature as I step in, and Nash follows me. His hands find my shoulders and stay there, just holding me while the water rinses over both of us. He presses a kiss behind my ear before reaching for the shampoo. I assume he'll hand me the bottle, but instead, he pours some into his own hand and starts washing my hair for me. He's a couple of inches taller than me, and I shamelessly lean into it.

It's hard not to think about how different this feels from my marriage. How much better.

When I asked my ex-wife for something I wanted—something I'd barely worked up the courage to say—she looked at me like what I'd said was disgusting instead of vulnerable.

I remember the pit in my stomach and the shame.

It made me feel like what I desired wasn't safe to want or okay.

Until now.

Until Nash.

He makes me feel safe and seen and cared for in a way I've never experienced before.

His fingers scrub circles in my hair and it feels incredible.

"Still good?" he asks, checking in.

I nod, swallowing thickly. "Yeah. I'm really good."

Nash's thumb brushes across my jaw as he turns me to face him. "Good. That's all I want for you."

Maybe this is what trust feels like—a small moment with someone you care about where you don't feel the need to keep your guard up, or feel like you're waiting for the other shoe to drop and bracing for impact. Where you can just be messy, vulnerable, and still figuring it out because your partner meets you with space instead of expectation.

Nash might not officially be my partner, but I really want him to be.

It already feels like he sees all of me, even the parts I was taught to tuck away. And instead of making me feel bad, he leans in. It's so fast, but he makes me feel like I can trust him, like he won't use my vulnerability against me or hold it hostage.

For fuck's sake, he came on my face, and then helped lick me clean.

That's not just trust. That's something else entirely. Something rare and real and once-in-a-lifetime.

I already know that if things don't work out between us, I'll never want another person the way I want him.

We finish the shower, and when we step out, cum-free, I

already feel different. More relaxed and more myself than ever before. And I feel like I have that thought after every single interaction with him.

Nash grabs my hand after checking to make sure none of the kids are lurking in the hallway, and he pulls me to our room with our towels wrapped around our waists. My face hurts from smiling at how fun sneaking around the cabin is with him.

How fun *everything* is with him.

We get to the bedroom and close the door behind us. Nash drops his towel and starts pulling on a clean pair of boxer briefs from his bag.

"As much as I'd love to feel your bare ass against me tonight, we should probably put some clothes on, just in case. Sometimes Em gets scared and comes in during the middle of the night if we're away from home."

"Makes sense," I say, pulling my own underwear out of my bag.

He crawls into bed and slides under the covers, lifting up my side for me to climb in. I do, and the minute I'm situated, he pulls me to him, spooning me, and we both just breathe for a second. My hand finds his, and I thread our fingers together between us.

He's quiet, and for some reason, I feel the urge to open up and share more of myself with him.

"It's been a long time since I felt... safe with someone, and I didn't know how much I missed it," I start.

He shifts closer, pressing a kiss behind my ear. "You are safe with me, baby. I'll always make sure of that."

I let out a small laugh. "God, I feel so ridiculous even saying that, but something about you just cracks me right open. Makes me feel like I can be vulnerable."

"I'm glad you trust me," he responds. "It sounds like maybe this is the first time you've ever truly been able to be your full self with someone, and I'm glad I get to see the real you."

I take a breath in, exhaling slowly. It feels easier to admit this in the dark with him wrapped around me from behind. "Yeah. It is. I've always hidden parts of myself. But with you, I don't feel like I need to hide or change because you make me feel safe enough to explore the desires I've kept hidden."

"Do you want to tell me about it?"

It's been a long time since I talked about my past, but it feels like right now, this is what I need to do.

"I grew up in small-town Missouri in a tight-knit, church-going, conservative community. My parents were… traditional, to put it nicely. I liked girls, but somewhere along the way, I realized I also started noticing guys. But I didn't realize it could be both because I didn't know being bi was a thing. You were either straight or you were gay. There was no in-between. And if you were gay, well… you better not be."

He wraps his arms around me fully, holding me tight.

I pause to catch my breath. "So I dated women, and had relationships I really cared about. I got engaged, and I wasn't faking that relationship. I did love her. I just kept the other parts of me locked down so deep I pretended they didn't exist, or tried. Your ex knew you were bi, but mine didn't. I feel like such a shitty person sometimes for not telling her, but I never felt safe enough to share that part of me. Then, after our divorce, it didn't feel right to start exploring myself because I was now a single parent. It felt scary, and I felt so far behind even though I knew I really wanted to try dating men."

I feel Nash exhale against my shoulder, his body curving

closer. "I'm really glad you're letting yourself explore this now."

"Me too, and I'm even happier it's with you," I say, swallowing down the rest... for now.

"Me too. I really like spending time with you and getting to know you," Nash responds, and I nod in his arms.

We lay there like that for a while—our legs tangled, the sheets pulled up around us, our fingers still locked together in front of my chest. Every now and then, one of us shifts to get more comfortable, but neither of us lets go.

And eventually, I feel him drift off, not far behind him.

And I think to myself—

I want nights like tonight again.

And again.

And again.

CHAPTER 18

Nash

I wake up feeling squished. There's a knee in my back and a tiny arm slung over my shoulder.

It takes me a second to remember where I am. I look down and see Emma sprawled out sideways between Caleb and me, the blankets pulled up over her, and she's snoring softly. I look over her to find Caleb's already awake, watching me behind his glasses with the kind of look that's equal parts affection and amusement.

"She came in sometime after midnight," he whispers. "Said she had a bad dream, and I figured it was fine since you told me this might happen, so I didn't wake you."

I nod, smiling at him. It's comforting to know he's naturally good with my kids and thoughtful, even when half asleep. Not everyone would've known how to handle that situation.

"Well, she's got great timing," I murmur, glancing down at her sleeping between us. "And I mean that literally. So glad we were clothed and asleep."

Caleb laughs under his breath, careful not to wake her. "Yeah, I had that same moment of panic."

I shake my head and look over at him. "You handled it perfectly," I say quietly. "If she didn't beg for me, she already trusts you, and that's huge. Thank you, Cay."

His eyes soften, and I don't think I've ever felt something hit me quite like that look. This right here—him in bed with me, talking quietly while my daughter sleeps between us—looks a lot like the future I've dreamed of.

We just smile at each other for a moment until Emma shifts again, rolling closer into Caleb's side, her tiny fingers gripping his arm. It's absolutely adorable, and Caleb doesn't seem to mind... because he's perfect.

"She's still out," he whispers, looking down at her.

"Thanks for being such an awesome dad, even with my kids."

"Of course, you all make it easy." He grins.

It's quiet for just a second before we hear loud footsteps barreling down the hallway and Sam and Benji bust into the room.

"Dad! We're hungry!" they both say in unison.

And now Emma is awake.

Caleb lets out a soft laugh as Emma stirs between us, blinking sleepily. "Perfect timing," I say, brushing a piece of hair out of her face. "Hey, Em. You want pancakes?"

She nods groggily, then climbs out of bed. We both get up and throw on T-shirts and pajama pants, and Emma immediately reaches for my hand. I take it without hesitation, and then she reaches for Caleb to take her other one. He does, and the sight of them together—her small fingers curled around his—makes me feel all gooey inside knowing she finds comfort in his presence.

"Come on, chefs," I say, leading the way to the kitchen. "Let's make breakfast. I brought stuff for pancakes and bacon."

"Yes!" Benji cheers, pulling the fridge door open to grab the bacon.

The kitchen turns into a happy kind of chaos as Benji and Sam measure the ingredients for the pancakes, which is just the mix and water, but they've managed to turn it into a two-man job. I make coffee for Caleb and me while he helps Emma wash the blueberries. Then I put the bacon in the oven.

"Bacon in the oven, huh?" Caleb asks, eyeing me suspiciously.

"It's so much easier, trust me. It cooks more evenly, and you don't have scorching hot grease splatters all over the kitchen. And, most importantly, no risk of the kids getting burned that way."

"You make good points, as usual," he says with a smile. "I'll have to try that next time."

"Batter's ready," Benji calls out.

"Alright, time for a tester pancake," I announce. "It's the most important one."

"Dad always does this," Emma tells Sam, and it's adorable that she wants him to feel included.

After the tester is good, we start on the real pancakes. Caleb is flipping them while I pick Emma up to drop the blueberries in the circles of batter as they sizzle. He's steady and patient, murmuring "Perfect, Em" each time she has the right amount. She beams at this praise, and I swear I feel it in my chest.

When the food is done, all five of us sit at the table, eating blueberry pancakes and bacon. As I eat, I take it all in—our kids, Caleb, the way none of it feels like something I have to manage, but something I get to enjoy.

Caleb catches my eye across the table. "What?" he asks, his brow quirking.

"Nothing." I smile. "This is nice. I'm happy."

His smile creeps across his face, and I can tell how much he's feeling it too. "Me too, and the bacon is good. I think you sold me on cooking it in the oven."

"I had a feeling I would."

ONCE BREAKFAST IS over and everything's cleaned up, we pack up from the night, load the cars, and head back to the mountain for more skiing.

By midday, we decide to call it quits and head back home. The kids are worn out from the morning and have somehow managed to turn who fell the hardest into a competition.

Meanwhile, I'm already missing Caleb, and we haven't even gotten into our cars yet to go our separate ways. My gut twists at the thought of saying another goodbye. I want one more night, one more morning, even if I'm already sure one more will never be enough.

As we start taking our gear off, I turn to him. "I'm glad this worked out. I know it was last minute, but this was another perfect weekend with you."

He shakes his head. "I wouldn't have missed it. Thank you for planning this and including us."

"You're the reason I planned this, Cay," I assure him, and his cheeks darken.

When we're finally out of our layers and ready to leave, he turns to face me. I want to kiss him again, but since we aren't there yet with the kids around, I settle for the next best thing and pull him forward into me.

"I'll text you when we're back," I murmur in his ear, quickly pressing a discreet kiss to his cheek.

He nods. "Please do."

My chest tightens as I watch him walk away from me to get into his car. I pull out of the parking lot first, and he follows right behind me, as we once again make our way back to reality.

I'm trying to shift my brain back into regular parent mode, but my fingers are still tingling from where they touched him, and I catch myself replaying last night and our conversations. I hate that Caleb has had to hide so much of himself in this life, and I know there's more he hasn't said, but I don't want to rush him.

Things were so different for me. I was in college when I hooked up with Brock, a guy from my communications class. There'd been some growing tension between us, and one night when we were drunk, I went back to his apartment with him, and we hooked up. I liked it enough that we did it a few more times, too.

And I was lucky, really lucky, because when I came out, I was met with nothing but love. I told my parents I was bi over Christmas break that year, and my mom hugged me, and my dad told me I was still the same person, just with more options. I had a feeling they'd be that way, which is why I knew I'd be okay sharing that part of me with them even though I was still nervous at the time.

When I went back to school for the spring semester that year, I met Tess, and we'd become inseparable. I told her about Brock, so there were no secrets between us, and she was completely cool with it too.

My sexuality has never been a secret for me because it didn't have to be, and I'm well aware not everyone is that lucky.

Knowing Caleb didn't have that same support makes me so angry. No one should have to feel unsafe in their own skin for loving who they love. And if I can be someone who makes it even a little easier for him to breathe, to exist, to explore… then I want to be that person. I want to walk beside him while he finds the version of himself that feels most like home. I just hope that version includes me.

"Dad! Look!" Benji shouts, breaking through my thoughts. I notice a hand-painted wooden sign staked into a snowbank.

`Cut-Your-Own Tree Lot. Five Miles Ahead.`

I glance in the rearview mirror at the kids, who are looking at me excitedly.

"You want to cut down our Christmas tree here?" I ask, knowing the answer.

"I want to!" Benji shouts.

"Me too!" Emma piggybacks.

"Perfect, let's do it! Thanks for pointing that out, bud. Let me make a quick call to see if Caleb and Sam want to join us."

I tap Caleb's name on the car screen in front of me and hit the call button. It rings once before I hear his perfect voice.

"Hey," he says. "Everything okay?"

"How would you feel about going with us to cut down a Christmas tree? We just passed a sign for one five miles down the road."

"I wanna go! Please, Dad!" I hear Sam say, followed by Caleb's laugh, knowing his phone must be on speaker too.

"Yeah, it sounds like we'll meet you there," he confirms in a warm tone.

"Can't wait, see you in a few minutes," I say eagerly.

Before I went rogue and booked the cabin, the plan had been to get our Christmas tree this weekend—drive out, find the perfect one, cut it down, then head home to decorate it with the Emma-approved Christmas playlist. I figured they'd be bummed when I told them we were delaying it, but there were no complaints when I surprised them with the trip, which is why it feels like the perfect way to end the weekend. We'll stop for a tree, bring it home, string up the lights, and maybe—if I'm lucky—I can convince Caleb and Sam to decorate with us too. I love it when a sporadic plan falls into place.

I glance back at the kids as I pull into the small gravel lot. There are more hand-painted signs and rows of Christmas trees dusted in snow. The kids perk up the second we park, and I help Emma get out. A minute later, Caleb pulls up beside us and steps out, his hair still messy from his helmet.

"Glad you wanted to do this with us," I say as he approaches.

"Anything for more time with you," he whispers before raising his voice. "Sam was clearly excited."

"We've never done this," Sam adds on, making his way toward where Benji is starting to take off toward the trees.

"Hey, Benj, let's go check in first."

He sighs, as expected, but follows us over to the small check-in booth with Emma and Sam. It's a little red shack with string lights, a chalkboard menu offering hot chocolate, cider, and mini donuts, with a couple of bundled-up teenagers sitting nearly on top of the propane space heater.

"Are you here for cut-your-own?" the girl asks as we approach.

"Yep." I nod, and she hands us a saw, a tree tag, and points toward the open rows.

"Great! Just pick your tree, cut it down, and bring it back here. We'll wrap it up for you. And don't forget to grab cocoa when you're done."

Caleb raises an eyebrow at me as we walk away, saw in hand. "Definitely going to need cocoa after this."

"I can make that happen." I chuckle and glance over at him. "So, do you still need a tree, or are you just helping us pick out ours?"

"Don't judge," he says. "But we've had a fake one up since November first."

I raise an eyebrow, glancing over at him. "Wow. So you're *that* house, huh?"

"Hey"—he nudges my shoulder as he walks beside me—"we like to celebrate early. It's our favorite time of the year. Besides, like I told you, it's just the two of us, so we decide when it feels like the right time, and it's usually the day after Halloween."

"I love that you have your own routines and traditions," I assure him as we turn down another row, Emma skipping ahead with Sam and Benji.

"Dad, what about this one?" Benji yells.

Sam points toward a different tree nearby. "This one's better! It's way fuller."

"Only because you can't see the back," Benji calls back.

"Okay, okay." I laugh, holding up my hands. "We'll inspect them all."

Emma tugs on Caleb's hand. "Caleb, should we get a tall one or a chubby one?"

My heart melts at how much she seems to be enjoying Caleb's presence. She's a pretty outgoing girl, but she's really taking a liking to Caleb, just like I have.

He crouches down to her level, pretending to consider very seriously. "Hmm. I think the fuller ones give better hugs. But tall ones make good climbing trees."

She gasps. "We can't climb the Christmas tree!"

"See? That's why a wide one might be better, if you have space for it in your house, that is."

She giggles, and I glance over just in time to catch the smile Caleb gives her, which is full of so much adoration.

"Dad!" Benji calls again. "We need a vote! Come see this one!"

"Duty calls," I say, making my way toward the next contender.

Caleb and Emma's shoes crunch in the snow behind me, and by the time we catch up, Benji is standing proudly beside a tree that's just a little taller than him, full on all sides.

"This one," he says confidently.

"I like it," Caleb agrees, running a hand along the needles.

Emma nods solemnly. "It looks like a tree that would like our ornaments."

Sam walks a slow circle around it, arms crossed, inspecting it. "I vote yes."

I take a few steps back to see it from all angles. It's not perfect, but it's exactly right. "Alright," I nod. "This one's coming home with us."

Caleb hands me the saw and helps hold the tree while I saw the base. The kids all cheer when it falls over, and I drag it through the snow to the counter we checked in at to pay.

There are a couple of guys who help net the tree before Caleb and I tie it to the roof of my car.

"We've got cocoa and cider if you want to warm up," the girl reminds us.

"Can we get some? Please?" Benji begs, and I give them a nod. They all take off toward the shop, and ten minutes later, we're all seated around a fire pit with warm paper cups in our hands, talking and laughing.

The perfect end to the perfect weekend.

CHAPTER 19
Caleb

Nash is waiting for me to call. He texted an hour ago to say the house felt too quiet without the kids since they're at their mom's house. I told him I'd let him know when I finish reading to Sam, who's nearly asleep but isn't ready to stop fighting it just yet. He's curled into my side, blanket pulled to his chin.

"Just one more page," he mumbles with barely open eyes.

"Alright," I whisper, flipping the page. My voice drops to a softer tone to read to him, and a minute later, his breathing finally evens out.

Even though I can't wait to talk to Nash, I stay by Sam's side a little longer, brushing my hand through his hair. These moments don't last forever. He won't always want me to read to him or sit in his bed with him or lean against me when he's tired. So I let my hand rest there for a bit longer, soaking it in before I go talk to the other person who's started taking up space in my heart.

When I finally slip out of bed and make my way down the hall to my room, I climb under the covers and call.

"Hey." Nash's voice beams through the phone.

"Hey, sorry that took so long. Sam wanted a second chapter of his book. Then a third."

Nash chuckles. "I don't mind. I like imagining you doing the bedtime thing."

"Oh yeah?" I tease.

"Yeah," he says with adoration in his voice. "Just you being you. Taking care of Sam. Being the best dad."

My eyes water slightly at that because being seen like this catches me off guard in the best way.

"So, what'd I miss over there?" I ask.

"Nothing at all." He sighs. "It can be nice to have the house to myself, but a lot of the time it just feels empty and lonely. I miss them when they're with their mom."

"Sometimes I wish I had someone to help me with Sam, but the thought of him not being here with me at all times also feels unimaginable."

"It's a double-edged sword, that's for sure."

I nod to myself as my mind drifts. For most of Sam's life, it's just been the two of us. I'm used to being the one who does everything, used to holding it all together. And I've never really let anyone else in—not past a certain point.

But Nash is different. He's gentle and thoughtful, and when I picture him here, it doesn't feel like a disruption to our lives. It feels right. He feels like the perfect addition.

"Hey, Nash," I start. "I just thought of something. Would you want to come over? You could stay the night. As long as you're okay with leaving before Sam wakes up?"

There's a pause on the other end of the line. "Yeah, of course," he says. "I'd love to, Cay, and we should probably talk about a few things anyways. Good things, I promise."

"Yeah," I say, my throat tightening unexpectedly once

again knowing he wants to talk more about us. "We should. Thank you."

"Send me your address, and I'll be over soon!" he says excitedly before hanging up, and I do.

The house is hardly dirty, but I panic clean anyway—remaking my bed, tidying up the bathroom to make sure I don't look like a slob. It only takes a couple of minutes, so I jump into the shower after to freshen up.

There's so much energy coursing through me, especially with the looming conversation we agreed to have. Are we talking about the kids? About what this is? What it might become? What if I come on too strong and he realizes he doesn't want to be with me? He said it was good things, but my mind is stirring with so many thoughts as I wait for him to get here.

About twenty-five minutes later, my phone lights up, and I reach for it quickly.

NASH:

I'm here.

I walk toward the door and tug it open to see Nash standing there in a hoodie and jeans, and he wraps me in a hug. His arms are strong and steady around my back, and I melt into his embrace until he pulls back to capture my mouth. It's the kind of kiss that feels like exhaling after holding my breath all day. It's hungry and desperate, and the second his hand comes up to cup the side of my face, I lean into it even more.

Even though he's kissed me before, this one feels different. He's here, at my house, ready to spend the night and hopefully try new things with me. I chase his lips for a second longer before I finally break away, breathing hard.

"Missed me, huh?" He grins, a little breathless.

"Obviously." I take his hand and lead him to my room. I feel equal parts giddy and nervous as usual.

Once we're in my room, I click the door shut behind us, and I pull him toward the bed. We both drop down, and Nash leans in again, and I meet him halfway. The kiss is slower this time. His hand cups my jaw again and mine slips beneath the hem of his shirt, fingers skating over the skin of his back.

But just as my heart starts pounding louder than my thoughts, I pull back.

"Wait," I pause, my palm resting on his chest now. "Before this goes any further, can we talk?"

He pulls back immediately, eyes searching mine. "Of course." He shifts so he's sitting in front of me and reaches for my hand. "I'm ready when you are. Where do you want to start?"

"Well, for starters, I haven't dated since the divorce," I admit, diving right into it. "And that scares me. Not just for me, but for Sam. If this gets messy—or if it doesn't work—I don't want him to get hurt. He's already been through one parent walking out."

Nash's face softens as he brushes his thumb across my knuckles.

"I get that," he says. "Believe me, I do. I'm always thinking about that line too—the one between what I want, and what's best for Benji and Emma. I think about what it means to bring someone into their world and how it'll affect them."

"But I like you," I blurt, hoping he knows that's where I was going with this. "A lot. And I think I just needed to say that out loud."

"I like you too." Nash grins back at me. "A lot. I think

about you all the time, Caleb. I know we've only just started getting to know each other, but I feel like you fit so perfectly in my life."

"So… what do we do?" I ask.

"Just keep moving at a pace that works for us." He shrugs. "I'd like to be part of your life in whatever capacity you'll have me. Sam's too. I don't want to do something casual, I want to be all in."

A sense of relief washes over me when I hear those words, and my face breaks out into a huge smile. "Me too," I agree, my cheeks burning up. "What do we tell the kids? Or when do we tell them?"

"We don't need to rush anything, still," Nash comforts. "When the time feels right, we'll talk to them. But for now, we can keep exploring and doing group activities with the kids. And if things don't work out like we want them to, we'll figure out what to tell them then too."

I nod, heart full. "Thank you. For communicating with me about it."

"I'm not sure I know how to be any other way," Nash says with a small smile.

I lean over and kiss him, letting him feel how grateful I am before the heat quickly builds between us. His tongue presses between my lips into my mouth, and I welcome him. I want more of him, and I immediately think back to how good it felt to have his cock in my mouth. The thought makes me moan as he yanks me into his lap, wrapping his arms around me as I lean forward.

My hips start grinding on top of him, and I can feel his erection under my ass. He told me he wanted me to be shameless with what I want, and I want to be, especially after he told me he's all in. I want to take everything he's offering, everything I'd spent so long pretending I didn't want. I want him to show me how good this can be.

His hands reach for my shirt, pulling it over my head, and I do the same to him. The second his shirt is off, he flips us completely, so I'm on my back on the bed, and he's on top of me, licking at my neck without sucking.

The urge to have him mark me is now rising, but I'm a dad; I can't walk around with a fucking hickey on my neck. Still, it doesn't stop me from tilting my head to give him better access as I grind up against him.

"Fuck, baby. You're really horny for me tonight, huh?"

"Yes. Please, touch me," I whine.

He wastes no time, pulling down my pants and boxer briefs, stripping me bare. He climbs back over top of me and grinds into me with his jeans dragging along my sensitive cock. The roughness feels incredible. I can't help but press my hips up into him, grinding, until he pulls away. I whimper at the loss.

"You're so sexy laid out, hard and aching, beneath me."

"I need more, please," I beg. Allowing myself to ask for everything I want.

"Lube?" he asks, and my eyes widen and my lips part. I forgot about the bedside table drawer and what's in there besides the lube.

"Don't be shy now. And if you don't have any, it's okay, my mouth works perfectly. We can always just do blowjobs."

"No, that's not it at all," I rush out. "It's in the nightstand next to you."

He leans over, still on top of me, and I wait as the drawer is pulled open.

"Oh fuck, baby. You're dirty, aren't you?" he says as he looks at me with a smirk, eyes dark with heat. He reaches into the drawer and pulls out my large silicone dildo with balls molded to the base. "Do you like to fuck yourself on this, Cay?"

I wasn't sure what I expected from him finding that, but it wasn't this level of desire.

"Yes," I admit.

He pulls out the bottle of lube next, setting it on the table.

"That's fucking hot. If I get you all warmed up with my fingers, will you show me how you like to be fucked?"

The way I could come from those filthy words leaving his lips. *Holy hell.*

Nodding is the only form of communication I think I'm capable of in this moment as he leans forward and grabs my bottom lip between his teeth, biting it. I hiss, but love the sharp, fleeting pain of him claiming me and taking what he wants.

"You want me to tell you what to do?"

I nod again.

He climbs off my lap to strip out of his clothes until he's naked in front of me. His long, thick, perfect erection is straining toward me. I haven't even had him inside me yet— in the hole I really want filled—and he's already a million times better than my dildo, I just know it.

"Touch yourself, let me see how you stroke your dick when I'm not here and you're thinking of me."

Whimpering at the tone in his voice, I wrap my dry hand around my cock and stroke. Rubbing the head first in a semi-circle, rotating my wrist before moving my fist down my shaft.

"Stop."

My hand immediately freezes, and I look at him, waiting for his next command.

"Fuck, that's a good boy."

His praise sends a jolt of pleasure through me that I've never experienced. "Ohhh, holy fucking fuck," I pant, and my dick twitches in my hand.

He smirks at the sight.

"I am really enjoying getting to know you, Caleb." He grins, and I have to take a deep breath to slow my pounding heart. "Now you want me to work you open with my fingers? My tongue?"

"God, yes, please," I say, nervous but so excited. "I just showered before you came over," I blurt out in case he was worried but didn't want to bring it up.

"I can smell the soap on your skin still," he coos as he leans down to inhale where my pubes are. Suddenly, I feel self-conscious. No one has ever done that before, but he doesn't stop. Instead, he moves to the side of my dick, mouthing at my sensitive skin until he reaches my balls. He sucks the left one into his mouth before moving to the right one. I groan at how good it feels to have his mouth there. His tongue drops lower, and he licks a stripe up from my taint. No one has ever touched me there before, but it feels magical.

"More, please," I grit out.

He wastes no time moving his tongue over the same sensitive skin, licking and kissing until I'm writhing, wanting his mouth to move up to my swollen cock or down to my needy hole—and he does. He dips lower and lower, and I instinctively pull my legs back against my chest to give him full access. The desire to have him there is far outweighing the slight embarrassment I feel being in this position, and the "fuck" that falls from his mouth in adoration confirms how badly he also wants this. Wants me.

He's lying in front of me now, and his hot tongue licks a single stripe over my hole.

I moan like the slut I am for him, and he goes right back to it, lapping at my hole. It's the best thing I've ever felt. I pull my legs back as far as they'll go because I'm desperate for more.

"Oh fuck, more. Please, more, more, more," I ramble.

This is everything, the exact thing I've fantasized about more times than I can count. But somehow so much better than I imagined. He starts eating me like I'm his last meal, shoving his wet, hot tongue into my hole, and I gasp at the sensation of being filled there. The only thing I've ever had inside me before is my fingers and my dildo, and his tongue is putting those to shame.

"That's my good, needy boy. Fuck, I love this."

I whimper as he reaches for the lube, not wanting him to stop but excited for what's coming next.

"Let me get your tight hole nice and wet with my fingers, then you can show me how good you fuck yourself on your toy," he growls as he pushes his first finger in me, and all the worry and concern floats away. Completely uncaring that I'm acting desperate, I start riding his finger, eager for any piece of him he'll give me.

"Jesus, baby," he says before adding another. "You like being filled, huh?"

"So much," I admit.

He pulls his fingers out before pressing three in, and my desperation only grows. This might be my first time with another man, but my hole's been filled plenty by me.

"I'm ready," I whine, nearly ready to come, and I don't want to without my ass being stuffed full of cock... even if it's fake.

He lubes up my dildo until it's dripping and hands it to me. Wasting no time, I adjust my position. I get up on my knees, ass facing him so he can watch fully, and slowly insert the tip into my stretched hole.

"Mmmm, yes, Cay. Show me how good you fuck yourself."

I turn and look at him over my shoulder. "Hold the base for me?"

Biting his lip, he nods and shifts to his knees behind me on the bed, holding the base so I can give him the full show. I sink down slowly and let out a gasp when I bottom out and feel his hand below my ass. Pushing back up, I ride the dildo and reach behind me to squeeze my ass cheek with one hand and stroke my dick with the other. When I look back to make sure he's enjoying himself, he's stroking his cock with his free hand too, glistening from the lube.

"Every time you use this when I'm not here, I want you to think of me, baby. You're so fucking sexy right now."

"Yes, yesss. Fuck, I will."

I ride the silicone, and my thighs start to burn as I continue to fuck myself on my toy. I moan repeatedly when my ass hits Nash's hand because I wish it was him touching me. Him fucking me.

"Uugh… mmm…" I groan at the idea, and I need it. The toy is fine, but it's not good enough when he's in this room with me. I wish it was his hard cock inside me. Want to be slamming down against him, feel his balls slap against me, want his cum dripping out of me.

"Will you fuck me?" I ask before I can second-guess myself. I'm moving my hips slower and more seductively now. "As great as my dildo feels, I'm desperate for the real thing. I need a real cock inside me."

He stops holding the dildo, pulling it out of me, and immediately brings his hand up to slap my ass. For a moment, I panic that it was too loud and it'd wake Sam up, but then I remember that Sam sleeps through thunderstorms and wakes up in the morning asking if it rained.

"You need *my* cock," he emphasizes. "Not *any* cock."

Jesus fucking Christ. The possession and the sting on my ass make me shiver and my skin breaks out in goosebumps. He's unknowingly fulfilling all my fantasies in the most natural way right now.

"Yes, *your* cock." Then I remember the very real problem we're about to have. "Uh, actually... I don't have any condoms since I haven't been with anyone in a really long time."

Rubbing his hand over my ass, he soothes the burn. "I was tested after the last time I was with someone, which was also an embarrassingly long time ago."

"Me too," I breathe. "I'm good. I want this, Nash, if you do. I want you to replace the dildo with your dick and fuck me if you're okay with it."

"Mmmm," he groans, letting go of his dick. "You're such a good boy when you beg for my cock like that."

I'm still on my knees with my ass facing him, and his hands slide around my throat, pulling me back to him until I can feel his erection pressed against my ass—right where I want him. I grind my hips, hoping he'll just somehow slip in, but instead, he squeezes my throat a little tighter, and I whimper at his show of dominance.

"You're sure you want me raw?" he checks, deep voice right next to my ear.

"Please, yes, please," I beg, a needy, withering mess in

anticipation that my dream man is considering making my fantasies of being fucked come true.

He quickly squirts lube in his palm and strokes himself, and before I even finish begging, his tip is nudging at my hole.

"Breathe for me," he instructs, and I do. "That's it, baby."

He pushes in on my exhale, and even though I just fucked myself on the dildo, it burns a little, but at the same time, it feels like I'm taking my first real breath in my life. I moan like I'm finally being given everything I've ever desired in life, and he mutters a curse under his breath.

"Fuck, you're tight," he moans, and I nod.

"Keep going," I grit out.

He continues slowly pressing into me, and when he eventually bottoms out, I let out a massive exhale before wiggling my hips slightly to commit this feeling to memory.

"You okay?" he checks.

I can't believe this is happening, that Nash is inside me. It feels so different than my dildo, infinitely better. They aren't even comparable, honestly.

"So good," I assure him.

Nash lets out a little grunt. "You like being filled? You want me to use your hole? Want me to fuck you like you fucked your toy?" he says as he starts pulling out before slamming back into me.

"Yes, yes, I want to be your little slut," I say the words out loud without thought, and I don't even care how needy I sound.

"God, the fucking mouth on you," he preens before pushing me down on all fours. "You want to be a little slut for me?"

"Yessss," I pant as I drop down onto my elbows, leaving my ass completely exposed to him.

He starts pounding into me at a brutal pace, and I'm moaning into the pillow in front of me, unable to contain myself. Nash's thick cock is infinitely better than my dildo—so good they don't even compare. He has one hand on my lower back and the other on my hip, and his grip is punishing. He's using me for his pleasure, while giving me exactly what I want, what I've always wanted—to be fucked good and hard.

"Your hole is so perfect. Swallowing my cock perfectly, like a good little slut."

The degradation does more for me than I can admit, and I reach for my dick to start stroking myself. I don't want to come yet, but I'm not going to last either when he talks to me like that.

He smacks my ass hard enough that it stings and the pain shoots through me, and I stop stroking myself before I blow my load.

"Did I tell you that you could touch yourself?" he snarls.

"No," I whine.

"That's right," he says, slowing his thrusts, but I'm so close, I need more. "Hands off."

I'm desperate for friction, but I want to please him more, so I grip the pillow in front of me and beg for whatever he'll give me. "Please more, please. Need more of your cock, please."

His hips still completely, buried deep as he leans over my back, breath hot against my ear.

"You want more?" he growls, the edge of control slipping from his voice. "Then you keep your hands to yourself and let me give it to you."

I nod frantically, face pressed into the pillow, trying to breathe through the ache of needing more of him.

"Tell me what you want," he demands, one hand still gripping my hip, the other sliding up my back to curl around the back of my neck, squeezing lightly.

"To come," I gasp. "And I want your cum. Fuck, yes, that. Come inside me."

Nash pulls back and slams into me, hard enough that I choke on the breath in my throat. My grip on the bed gets tighter as he sets a punishing rhythm, every thrust pushing me further out of my head until the only thing I can think of is him and how badly I want him to make me come.

"Fuck, you take it so well," he grits out, voice tight and filthy. "My little slut is so fucking needy for my cum."

I moan loudly because I am. I've never felt like this before: split open, completely owned, and so unbelievably satisfied.

"That's my good fucking boy. Love hearing you moan like this while I fuck your gaping hole, baby."

CHAPTER 20
Nash

M other of fucking god.

This is the man of my dreams.

The dirty, filthy, sexy, slutty man of my dreams.

I yank him up by the back of his neck, turning his head to face me so I can slam my mouth to his just for a second before shoving him back down. He goes easily, falling back to his elbows, ass up and still full of my cock.

This man is everything, and the grip his ass has on me could make me come any second, but I don't want it to end. I thrust my hips slower now, teasing him to draw this out for both of us.

"Such a good hole for me, you know that, baby?"

He whines into the pillow, face buried again, and as much as I want to see his handsome face—and as affectionate as he is outside the bedroom—I can see how much he wants this. Wants to be used, to be told what to do, to be fucked like he deserves, and to be taken care of—and I want to be the one to give him everything.

"Nash, fuck, please. I want to come... Can't take it anymore."

The need in his voice, the sheer desperation, has me ready to finally give him what he wants, what we both want.

"I'm gonna finish in your ass," I grit out as I fuck him relentlessly. "Such a good boy for me, and good boys get rewards. Your tight little hole is going to make me come."

"Please," he begs.

"Touch yourself," I command, finally telling him what he wants to hear.

Almost immediately, his hole clenches tightly around me, spasming as his body jerks. I groan, giving in. My cum spills deep inside of him as I hold him still, buried to the hilt, letting him milk every last drop from me while he moans through his orgasm, cock twitching in his fist as he comes across the sheets.

He slumps forward more, breathing hard, his body trembling slightly with aftershocks, and I follow him down, not ready to let go just yet. I stay inside him, my chest pressed to his back, and my arm curling around his waist as I kiss the back of his neck.

"You okay?" I murmur, voice rough with the force of it all.

He nods against the pillow, then glances back at me with a dazed, blissed-out smile. "More than okay."

I press another kiss between his shoulder blades and hold him there, letting the heat of our bodies settle until I'm ready to pull out of him. The moment I do, I scoot back enough to watch my cum slowly leak out of his ass, and I'm obsessed with the sight. I take two fingers and push it back in, and he whimpers again.

"I wish you could see your used hole with my cum dripping out of you. It's perfect. You are fucking perfect."

He turns his head to look up at me, eyes still glassy. "Really?" he asks with a hint of disbelief in his voice, and I pull my gaze away from his body to comfort him.

I ease my touch over his side, letting my hand rest gently on the curve of his hip as I meet his eyes. "Yeah," I murmur, softer now. "Really. You're—Jesus, you're everything."

He swallows, cheeks pink, and I know what we just did was a lot. I've never gone that far with someone, in terms of speaking that way. But the way he responded, the way he opened up to me, clung to me—wanted me—I'd do it all over again. I want to do it all over again.

"Wanna hop in the shower?" I ask, brushing his sweaty hair off his forehead. "We're kind of a mess."

He nods at me, and I kiss the corner of his mouth, then slip off the bed, and head into the bathroom to turn the water on. When I come back, he's still curled on the bed. I lean over him, and start kissing his face—his cheek, his temple, his jaw —until he lets out a breathy laugh.

"Come on." I grin, gripping his fingers. "Should be hot by now."

He hesitates, shifting a little, and I worry he's self-conscious about the mess between his legs. Instead of grabbing a towel or making it a thing, I just bend down and open my arms. "Let me carry you."

"You're ridiculous," he says, but there's that smile again, and he loops his arms around my neck anyway.

I pick him up, and he's lighter than I was expecting. I shift him in my arms as he wraps his legs around me, and I slide my fingers gently over his hole to catch the slow leak of my cum before gravity works against us. He tenses slightly as he realizes what I'm doing, but he doesn't say anything.

I take a few steps into the bathroom and set him down in front of the shower, letting him stand on his own, and trail my hand down his back one last time before stepping in behind him.

"How was that, baby? Was it okay for your first time?"

He huffs a little laugh. "It's like you hacked into my porn search history and knew exactly what I wanted. Except it was somehow better. Way better," he confesses, and I immediately feel at ease. He was enjoying himself during it, but sometimes the comedown can be hard, and hearing him say that eases any concern I had.

"I'm glad," I murmur, trailing my fingers along his hip. "I told you I wanted you to be honest about what you want, and I meant it. Was there anything that didn't feel right? Anything you want more of next time?"

He pauses, then shakes his head. "It was perfect. Though, I wouldn't be opposed to more ass slapping or your hand around my neck. I really liked that; it felt like you owned me."

I nod because I can do that. "What about me calling you a slut?" I check. Even though he'd said it first, it's definitely not something I'm used to saying during sex, and I want to make sure I gave him what he wanted without crossing any lines.

He groans softly, eyes fluttering shut for a second as his cheeks turn red. I've noticed how easily he blushes, and I love that.

"Especially that," he assures me. "I've jerked off to fantasies like that, but nothing compares to what it felt like with you. I really liked you taking control and being dominant like you were."

Relief and satisfaction hit me hard in the chest at his answers as I wash him. I'm careful with his skin, gentle now in all the places I'd been rough with earlier.

"Do you have an extra set of clean sheets I can grab?" I ask, kissing his shoulder.

"In the closet on the top shelf."

"Stay in the hot water while I change the bed," I tell him. "I want you warm."

After I've dried off and tossed the sheets in the hamper, I spread out the clean ones and let him know the bed's ready for him. He steps out of the bathroom, damp and flushed, with his cute-as-fuck glasses on. I wrap him in a fresh towel before pulling him toward the bed.

Once we're under the covers, I drag him into my chest with his back pressed tight to me like we were always meant to fit this way. My fingers brush over his stomach, loving the feel of him tucked in close to me.

"I set my alarm for five thirty, does that work for you?"

"Yeah," he says quietly. "I wish you could stay longer, but I know why we're waiting. Sam usually doesn't wake up until a few hours after that."

There's something in his voice that makes me want to promise I'll never leave at all. But we're still figuring this out, and as much as I feel that promise to be true, I can't say it just yet.

"Perfect," I murmur, pressing a kiss to the space behind his ear. "Thank you again for inviting me over tonight. I needed this. You."

He hums, nuzzling into the pillow.

"There's one more thing," I add gently. "I have a work Christmas party this weekend, and I'd love you to come with me if you're free. It's Friday night at six, at a hotel downtown.

We could stay over, make a night of it—or go for a few hours, whatever works for you."

He shifts slightly to look at me, sleepy but touched. "I'd love to. Let me figure something out for Sam, but yeah… I'd really like that."

I smile into his hair. "That sounds great."

I might have an idea for who could watch Sam, but I don't want to bring it up right now while he's so happy and sleepy. He exhales and snuggles in closer until he's fully tucked into my chest. I wrap my arm tighter around him, my thumb tracing small circles on his side.

Just like I have the last two times with him, I fall asleep knowing I'm exactly where I want to be and with the person I want to be with.

CHAPTER 21

Caleb

I can't remember the last time I felt this nervous.

Sam is in the backseat, chatting about what kind of snacks he hopes Benji's mom has. I'm nodding along, but my brain is off doing its own thing. Because, yep, we're going to Tess's house—Nash's ex-wife—so I can meet her, and Sam can sleep over with Benji and Emma.

This definitely wasn't on my bingo card for this week, but Nash suggested that since Emma and Benji would be with her tonight, Sam should join for a sleepover while we go to his company Christmas party. He said he had already run it by her, and she was "cool with it." I hate to admit I'm struggling to comprehend how they're *this* cool with each other, that it's not a big deal that I'm dropping my son off at my maybe-boyfriend's ex-wife's house for a sleepover.

At that point, I couldn't help myself; I had to ask Nash point-blank why they got divorced if they still get along so well.

He said they got married right after college and eventually realized what they had wasn't romantic love anymore. That they cared about each other, but more in a friend way than an "I can't live without you" way, and that ultimately, they decided they each deserved more. It sounded like a completely amicable decision.

"We respected each other enough to let go so we could each figure out who we really were," he told me.

I've been turning that over in my head since he said it because that kind of mutual, communicative, and understanding ending is so far from how my marriage ended. With my ex, it was passive-aggressive silences and hateful words. It was losing little pieces of myself over time until she decided she was done with me. She walked away, leaving me feeling confused and convinced that something was wrong with me. It still breaks my heart for Sam's sake. Hating me is one thing, I can live with it, but to abandon Sam? I didn't understand that and never have. He deserves so much better.

I'm glad Nash and his kids didn't have to deal with that, and that he has someone so supportive, even after their divorce. Someone who gave him the freedom to further explore himself without shaming him.

We pull up at the address Nash sent me. It's a white house with brick around the door and a covered porch. It's a standard Denver house, and the normalcy makes me feel slightly better.

Sam unbuckles and opens the car door excitedly, running up the porch while I quickly text Nash that we're here.

"Can I ring the doorbell?" Sam asks, looking back at me.

"Go for it." I force a smile and try to channel even a fraction of his excited energy, but all I feel is anxious. I walk up to the porch with my hands jammed into my coat pockets, silently praying this won't be weird.

A moment later, the door opens, and Tess is standing

there. Her brown hair is pulled back into a ponytail. She's wearing glasses, leggings, and a sweatshirt, and she's beautiful. Nash steps behind her, and my stomach instinctively sinks at the look of the two of them together. They look... great. They look like they're meant to be together. But I know that's just my own insecurities playing tricks on me.

"Hey, you must be Sam," Tess says warmly. "Come on in, the kids are playing in the living room."

Sam gives her a polite "Hi, thanks" before kicking off his shoes and sprinting toward the sound of Emma and Benji's voices somewhere in the back of the house.

Meanwhile, I hang back awkwardly on the porch.

"Hey, Tess," I say, awkwardly sticking out my hand to her.

She chuckles and shakes it. "You must be Caleb. It's nice to finally meet you and not just hear your name in stories. You've really got this one down bad," she jokes, nodding her head in Nash's direction.

"What can I say? He's great. And so handsome, just look at him," Nash compliments, like I'm not standing right here, and my face feels like it's on fire.

"See what I mean? Down bad," Tess jokes. "Want to come in? Have a drink before you guys head out?"

"Sure, that sounds good," I answer, stepping into the house as Tess turns and walks down the hall toward what I assume is the kitchen.

"It's all going to be okay," Nash whispers as he pulls me in for a hug and gives me a quick kiss.

I smile, kick my shoes off, put Sam's bag by the door, and follow Tess and Nash into the house.

"I should've clarified; I don't have anything alcoholic, but I do have some sparkling water."

"That's perfect, thanks."

Nash sits at the dining table, so I take his lead and do the same.

Tess moves around the kitchen, grabbing a glass and pulling a can from the fridge.

"Here you go," she says, sliding the drink on the table.

"Thanks." I take it, noticing how relaxed Nash looks in her kitchen.

Tess sits across from me, and for a second, it hits me how strange this all is. Yet, somehow, it feels good knowing that she really does seem to support us.

"You okay?" Nash leans toward me slightly, voice low.

"Yeah," I say quickly.

I look around the room, taking it all in. Family photos line the wall, a mix of kid drawings and vacation snapshots. Nash is in a couple, and I try not to feel weird about it because I do trust him.

"How's work been?" Tess asks Nash, pulling my attention back to the table.

He shrugs. "Busy, but manageable. End-of-year stuff."

"Are you excited to meet his coworkers?" she asks me.

"Yeah, a bit nervous about that too. But probably not as nervous as I was to come here, honestly," I say with a self-deprecating laugh.

"But you did it, and now you never have to meet me for the first time again." She laughs, and I'm relieved I didn't make it weird between us.

"I can't believe you two still get along so well. When Nash told me, I was shocked," I admit.

"Well, he was my best friend as soon as we met, but that didn't give either of us time to figure out who we are on our own. We realized we always did act more like best friends than romantic partners, which is why it's so good to see Nash this happy. I'm glad he met you," she says easily with no undertone of jealousy or spite.

"Thanks," I say before Nash can speak. "I really appreciate that."

Tess gives a small, understanding nod, and we talk for a bit longer before I say goodbye to Sam so we can head to the Christmas party.

"Call me if you need anything at all, okay, bud?" I instruct as I hug him.

"Okay, bye, Dad!" he rushes out, pulling away before I'm ready.

"Have fun, and be good for your mom," Nash tells the kids before we both turn and walk out the door.

I LIED. I might be equally as nervous about this Christmas party.

The hotel comes into view, and it feels like my heart is trying to climb out of my chest. The building is modern and tall, all sleek glass and warm lights glowing against the winter night. My palms are already damp, so I rub them against the fabric of my slacks, trying to steady myself.

Beside me, Nash leans in and presses a soft kiss to my cheek at the red light before we turn into the parking lot, like he can sense the shift in my breathing.

"This'll go great," he says quietly, and I believe that he believes that. Meeting Tess was one thing, but now that we're here, I think I underestimated how big of a deal this will be too.

When he shifts the car into park, I hesitate. My hand hovers over the seatbelt buckle as I stare out the windshield. I can feel the question rising in my throat, and I blurt it out before I lose my nerve.

"Hey, Nash, uh…" My voice wobbles, so I clear it and try again. "What should I say if someone asks who you are to me?"

The question hangs between us, and I feel ridiculous for asking it in my mid-thirties, but it's been gnawing at me since he invited me to this party. I've run through the scenario in my head a hundred times: Nash getting pulled into a conversation while I linger nearby, some colleague wandering over, asking who I am and what I'm doing there. I feel lost over such a simple question, fumbling, trying not to say the wrong thing. I don't know what Nash's coworkers know about him outside of work, or if he's out at work. And I don't want to say something that catches him off guard or unintentionally outs him.

Nash's eyebrows lift, then soften with understanding.

"Oh, baby," he soothes. "Is that why you've been so tense? I thought it was about leaving Sam with Tess for the night."

I exhale a quiet laugh. "No, I think that went well, and he'll be just fine."

"You can tell people I'm your partner. Or your boyfriend," he adds in a warm tone. "If you're more comfortable with that."

I blink at him as the b-word echoes in my head. "You want to be my boyfriend?"

Nash smiles so softly, and sure, and *him*.

"I'd be honored to be your boyfriend," he assures me. "If you'll have me."

I'm stunned silent for half a second, then I nod, a slow grin spreading across my face. "Yeah. I want that."

"Good. I was hoping you'd say that, Cay." He winks.

We climb out of the car, and the night air hits my face. Nash rounds the front of the car and meets me on the passenger side. He cups my face with both hands, the heat of him a stark contrast to the winter air. He leans forward and kisses me, respectfully, of course, since we're at his company work party.

When he pulls back, he rests his forehead lightly against mine.

"Come on, boyfriend," he murmurs, threading his fingers through mine. And just like that, the weight in my chest eases as we walk hand in hand toward the hotel entrance together. The night is dark and cold, snow is lightly falling from the sky, and it feels like the perfect night with the kind of magic only December can bring.

Inside, the lobby glows with soft lighting and garlands wrapped around banisters. A towering tree stands near the front desk, decked out in white lights and matching, themed ornaments.

Nash pulls me up to the counter with him while he slides his card across to the concierge and checks us in. They hand us two key cards and promise our bags will be sent up to the room shortly.

Once we've checked in, Nash leans close again, lips brushing my temple. "Ready?"

I exhale and nod. "Let's do it."

He holds my hand as he walks us to the Elkwood Ballroom. It's clear Nash wasn't exaggerating about the fact that his company goes all out for their holiday party. People in sleek suits and cocktail dresses mingle near multiple fully stocked bars as waitstaff weave through the crowd with trays of champagne and bite-sized hors d'oeuvres.

Nash gives my hand a quick squeeze as we walk in. "Still good?"

"Barely," I mutter. "This is amazing."

He chuckles softly, and before I can soak in another second, a man in a navy suit spots him from across the room and makes a beeline over.

"Nash!" the guy says, clapping him hard on the back. "Hey, man!" Then his eyes flick to me. "Hey, I'm Marshall," he says, reaching to shake my hand.

"Caleb. Nice to meet you," I respond, shaking his hand.

"You here with this guy?" he asks, clearly trying to place me.

"Guilty," I say with a shy smile, unsure how this conversation will go.

But it's... fine. Easy, even. We chat for a few minutes before even more people approach Nash, and introductions blur.

There's a guy dressed like an elf who I'm told does HR. Emily, the support director, raises a brow and breaks into a big smile when Nash introduces me as his boyfriend. Nash is relaxed and charming around his coworkers, and it's helping me be more comfortable too—especially since this is my first time *out* in public with a man. With my *boyfriend*.

Being at my boyfriend's work holiday party feels overwhelming in a good way, because I still can't believe this is my reality. It's going to take some time for me to comprehend that this is real, and we're actually dating.

Eventually, Nash pulls us toward a quieter corner with two flutes of champagne. "Surviving?"

"Yeah, just don't expect me to remember anyone's name," I huff out with a laugh.

"Of course not." He chuckles, leaning in closer now with his hand on my tie. "You look good, by the way."

I glance down at my dark green tie, then back up at him. "You just like that I'm wearing something you can tug on."

He smirks. "You're not wrong, baby."

I roll my eyes, but I'm smiling.

He nudges his shoulder against mine. "Thanks again for coming. This was so much better with you here."

"Thanks for inviting me," I whisper, eagerly awaiting the part where we can go upstairs.

Before I can respond, someone calls out his name and waves him over. He groans quietly. "Ready?" he asks, lacing our fingers together.

"Lead the way."

CHAPTER 22

Nash

The party winds down later than expected. A few of my coworkers are already plotting which bar to hit next, but I have a man who's free for the night, and I intend to take full advantage of that.

"You ready to get out of here?" I ask, leaning into Caleb.

He nods, relief in his smile. "God, yes. Please."

We trade goodbyes with a few people and make our way upstairs, hands linked as we walk through the fancy hotel lobby. When we get to the fifteenth floor and find our room, I slide the keycard into the door, and it clicks open with a soft beep.

We step into a room with a king-size bed, crisp white sheets, and a massive window wall overlooking the city, the lights glowing beneath us.

Caleb steps up toward the window in awe. "Wow. That's a nice view."

I step up behind him, wrapping my arms around his waist and pulling him flush to me. "Not as nice as what I'm looking at."

He leans back into my chest slightly, his head tipping to the side like he's offering me his neck, and I press a kiss there.

"Now we get the night to ourselves."

"Mmm, don't get those often."

"No, you don't, so tonight's all about you, Cay."

"I brought my lube." He grins over his shoulder at me.

My dick starts to perk up at the mention. I haven't stopped thinking about what we did the last time we were together—the way he fell apart for me, the way he begged for more, the way he was my own little personal and perfect slut. My desire for him is burning through my veins, the need is pooling low and hot in my gut, and I can't wait to fuck him tonight.

"Mmm, good boy," I praise. "There's no place hotter than a hotel room, is there?"

Looking around, he shakes his head, because there really isn't.

Reaching out, I cup his jaw, turning his mouth toward me. His stunning pale blue eyes with hazel specs look back at me, wide and waiting, already a little dazed from anticipation as I pull him into me. Our lips crash together as I make it known how much I want him, spinning him around until we're facing each other. Our bodies press together tightly, my thigh slips between his, and he starts grinding down against it, needy little sounds spilling from him as I devour his mouth.

When I pull back, his pupils are blown wide. I yank at his tie, the silk slipping through my fingers. "Shirt off, baby," I murmur, "but keep this on."

He obeys without a word, unbuttoning his shirt with an urgency that makes my blood run hotter. I kick off my shoes and shrug out of my shirt, keeping my eyes locked on him the entire time. He's standing in front of me with nothing but his slacks and that damn tie as his chest rises and falls fast, awaiting my next command.

I need him naked, though. Now.

Stepping up to him, my fingers slide over his waistband before I tug at his belt, undoing the clasp. The clink of the buckle makes him shiver, and I unfasten his pants, letting them drop to the floor. My gaze devours every inch of him as he stands there in just his briefs and tie now, already hard and waiting for me.

"You are so damn sexy, Cay," I growl, eyes roaming his body.

He looks up at me with a smile that's part shy, part hungry. I grab his tie, pulling him into me as our mouths crash together again. My other hand trails down, cupping his erection through the thin cotton of his underwear. He lets out a sharp breath, hips jolting forward, and I grin against his mouth as an idea strikes me.

"You want me to fuck your tight hole with the curtains open? Let everyone in Denver see how good you take my cock?"

His eyes flick to the glass then back to me as he swallows and nods. "Yes."

"Mmm," I groan. "Such a good boy for me. Everyone out there gets to see your perfect, hard dick leaking for *me* while I fuck you. How fucking lucky are they?"

He licks his lips, eyes shining. When I glance down, sure enough a damp spot is already forming through his boxer briefs at the thought.

"In front of the window," I order, my voice darker now. "Hands on the glass. Ass out."

He turns slowly, taking a couple of steps toward the wall

of glass. He plants his palms against it, arching his back, offering himself to me in the glow of the city night.

And fuck, the view has nothing on him.

I stalk up behind him, drag my hands slowly down his back, then lower until I hook my fingers into the waistband of his underwear. I peel them down inch by inch, revealing his round ass that's begging for me. When I tap his thigh, he steps out of them, leaving him gloriously bare except for the silk tie hanging from his neck.

I grip his hips and grind my still-clothed cock against his ass. He hisses at the friction, pushing back into me like he can't get close enough. I'm addicted to how he's surrendering so fully, letting himself want this while I take every inch of him I crave.

"Spin your tie around," I growl, wanting it where I can grab it.

He does instantly, so the tie trails down his back like a leash. I wrap it around my hand and yank it gently, pulling his head back toward me. The visual of him—naked, bent over, spine curved with his ass out and the city lights kissing his skin—is fucking art.

"Perfect," I breathe, voice laced with hunger. "God, you're fucking perfect."

I stop rutting against him just long enough to drop to my knees and sink my teeth into the swell of his right cheek. He gasps at the sensation, and the sound shoots straight to my cock. I soothe the bite with a slow, wet lick, grinning when he lets out a low, desperate whimper.

"You like that?"

"Yes," he pants. "Yes, please more. Please."

I press a kiss to the base of his spine, then look up at the flushed, trembling man in front of me.

"Good boy," I murmur. "Don't hold back. I want to hear everything. And if anything feels off or too much, you tell me. Understood?"

"Yes. Yes, Nash," he whimpers, voice wrecked already, and fuck, I love him like this—eager, needy, trusting.

I don't tease him or make him wait. He gave me the perfect answer, and good boys get rewards.

I dive right in, licking a stripe over his hole. His whole body jolts at the contact, hips rocking forward instinctively before he forces himself back into position. I hold him open with both hands and eat him out with purpose. Slow at first, then faster, deeper, until I'm devouring him. His thighs start to tremble, and his groans get louder and filthier.

"Fuuuck," he cries out, pressing into the window. "Oh my god."

I grin into him, spitting once and going right back to it, watching his back arch as I circle his hole and then press my tongue inside. The way he writhes under me is everything.

He gasps again, breath stuttering. "More... Fingers. I need —please."

I pull back just enough to speak, my voice thick with heat. "Your hole that desperate to be filled?"

"Mm-hmm," he whines, looking over his shoulder with dazed, glassy eyes. "Please."

"Where's the lube, baby?" There's no chance I would've shown up tonight without bringing a bottle of my own, but since he came prepared, I want to use his.

"Front pocket of my bag," he pants.

"Good," I growl, giving his ass a slap before standing. "Stay just like that."

At his bag, I unzip the front pocket, and the lube is the only thing inside. My good little planner. I grin, palming it before stripping off the last of my clothes. Now the only piece left between us is Caleb's tie that's hanging down his back, loosened slightly and ready to be pulled.

Before I return to him, I quickly duck into the bathroom and twist the oversized tub's faucet on, letting the water slowly drip out in preparation for after, as he stands there with his ass out waiting for me to touch him. It might overflow, but hopefully not with how slow I turned the drip on with the size of the tub. And it's more important to me that he feels taken care of after.

I make my way back to him, coming up from behind, coating my fingers in lube, and running them slowly over his hole. He shudders beneath my touch, already worked up from being empty. I press in with my pointer finger, and his body opens around it instantly, greedily, pushing back like he can't wait another second. His untouched cock is straining hard between his legs.

He takes one hand off the window and moves like he's going to grab it, but I yank his tie, stopping him. "Did I tell you to touch yourself?"

He lets out a sharp breath. "No."

"Then don't."

"But I—" He cuts off with a moan when I twist my finger, loosening him further. "Need more… just fuck me, pleaseee."

God, he sounds so beautiful and desperate and *mine* when he begs for my cock like that.

I slide in a second finger, working him open. I release my grip on his tie to reach for the lube again, slicking my cock up the best I can while he begs against the glass. His body is so responsive as his hips press back to meet every movement.

Before I pull my fingers out, I grab his tie again, winding

the silk tight around my fist and yanking gently so his head tilts back.

"I'm gonna fuck you now," I murmur into his ear, voice gravel and heat. "Okay, baby?"

He nods hard, panting. "Yes. Yes, please... Do it."

"Hands on the window," I command, mouth next to his ear. "And don't move them. Let everyone see how fucking pretty you are when you're getting split open on my cock."

He lets out a soft, broken whimper, but I want him even louder.

I push into him in one brutal thrust, burying myself to the hilt. His gasp echoes against the glass like he can finally breathe again as his back arches deeper, his perfect body welcoming me in like he was made for this.

"Fuck," I groan, one hand clamped tight around his hip. "You take my dick so well. My perfect little slut."

His muscles tense around me, clenching like he never wants to let go. I angle slightly to the side. My pace is unforgiving, with each hand on his hips, each thrust pressing him forward as the view of Denver is vast below us in the dark night.

I pull my hand back and land a sharp smack to his ass.

He cries out, but it melts into a moan. "Again," he gasps, voice desperate and thin.

I oblige. Again. And again. The sound of skin against skin echoes through the room, and his ass turns a deeper red beneath my hands. He shifts slightly, chasing the next strike.

"I wish you could see yourself right now," I growl, slowing my thrusts down ever so slightly. "Bent over, cock dripping, begging for more. You look fucking perfect taking my cock like this. Like such a good boy."

He's panting under me. "So... good," he gasps out, hips trembling.

My hand snakes around his front and finds his heavy balls. I cup them gently at first, then give them a sharp tug that makes him whimper and clench even tighter around me. His ignored cock is leaking and swollen, but I don't give him relief. I want every bit of his pleasure to come from being full of me.

"Is my little slut gonna come on my cock?" I murmur, fucking him deeper now. "Gonna make a mess without a single touch?"

"Yes—mmm, yes, harder," he pants, voice cracking with need.

I grunt, releasing his balls and grabbing his hips with both hands so I can drive into him harder, deeper, faster to give him everything he wants. The sound of skin slapping skin is the only noise in the room apart from our heavy breathing and pleasure-filled groans.

"There!" he cries out, head tipping back. "Right there, fuck, Nash—don't stop."

I've found the spot. The one that makes his whole body tremble, his thighs shake, and his ass pushes back like he can't get enough. I fuck him right there against the window for anyone to see, just like he begged for, basking in the way his body unravels for me.

"Need... Fuck, need to touch myself. Please, let me—"

"Go ahead, baby," I growl into his ear, "come while I fuck you right here in front of all of Denver. Let them see how desperate you are for me. How much of a pretty little slut you are when you're taking my cock."

He whimpers and removes one hand from the glass, wrapping

it around his leaking dick with urgency. He strokes himself in time with my thrusts, and within seconds, his whole body seizes, and he cries out as his orgasm hits. Hot cum paints the glass in front of him in thick pulses. And the second I feel his hole clench around me, milking my cock like it never wants to let go, I lose it.

"Fuck—Cay," I groan, sinking deep and stilling as I empty into him, filling him with my release.

My arms wrap tightly around his waist, holding him there while we both gasp for air. His head falls back against my shoulder, still panting, and I can feel the aftershocks rippling through him.

"Jesus," he breathes, voice shaky and sweet and ruined.

My cock is still inside him as I pull him to my chest. My hand slides up, fingers tilting his jaw until I can kiss him. It's full of passion and everything I don't know how to say out loud. *Thank you. You're perfect. I've got you. I can't believe I found you. Can't believe you're mine.*

When we finally break apart, he's still panting, and he lets out a soft noise as I finally slide free from his body.

He's flushed and marked and mine.

"Come on, baby," I whisper, brushing the hair off his forehead. "Bath's probably ready; let's get you cleaned up."

I hold out my hand, and he takes it, fingers curling around mine as I guide him toward the bathroom. I'm relieved to see the oversized tub filled just enough and not overflowing. Before I let him get in, I touch the water to make sure it's not too hot, but it feels perfect.

"Okay, you can climb in. I'll get in behind you."

He glances back at me with a teasing tilt to his lips, undoing the tie still hanging loose around his neck and tossing it onto the tile floor. "You better," he says with a smirk, then steps in and lowers himself slowly into the water, groaning at the heat.

I follow him, settling in with my legs framing his, chest against his back. He leans into me, his body relaxing as the warmth seeps into both of us. For a few quiet moments, we just breathe, the soft rising and falling of our chests syncing up as my arms come around his waist, and he rests his hands over mine.

"Nash?" he says softly.

"Yeah, baby?"

"Thank you. For everything." He pauses for a moment, and I give him space. "I've always dreamed of sex like this, and I never thought I'd get it. I guess I thought I'd waited too long. Or that maybe I was too old or too far behind or just... I don't know, it's dumb, but—"

"No, don't say that. It's not dumb. Not at all. If it feels good and we both like it and want it, that's all that matters."

He nods slowly, fingers trailing down my thigh, lingering there like he's still deciding whether to say more.

"I didn't mean to cut you off," I murmur. "What is it? I want to know."

"I haven't told you why I got divorced, have I?" he asks, and I pause because we haven't talked about this, or his ex at all, really. And I'm dying to know.

"No, you haven't."

"It's not something I like to bring up," he says, voice quieter now. "And I've never really been honest with anyone about why we got divorced. Even though I know it's for the best, and I don't miss her at all."

I don't interrupt him, just slide my arms tighter around his chest, holding him close so he knows I'm right here, listening.

"It's embarrassing," he admits, and I press a kiss to the

back of his head, hopefully comforting him and giving him strength. "Even though I know it shouldn't be."

He breathes in deep and steadies himself before continuing.

"I'd never been with a man before you, like I told you, but it's something I thought about a lot," he starts. "My ex and I didn't have a very active sex life, so she was okay with me watching porn. I was always drawn to videos with two guys and a girl, but only if the guys were into each other too. If they didn't fuck, it just... didn't do the same thing for me, and it felt like having the woman there made it okay."

He pauses, and I stay quiet, letting him get it out.

"I always knew she was more vanilla when it came to sex, but I figured... since we were married, maybe I could finally be honest about what I wanted to try in bed, but I was wrong."

I pull him tighter, resting my chin on his shoulder as he goes quiet again. This story is going to break my heart, I can feel it already, but I let him take his time.

"Anyway"—he exhales—"one night we were talking about trying to revive our sex life, and after working up the courage for what felt like forever, I asked her if she'd be open to pegging me, and she blew up on me. At that point, I'd only used my fingers occasionally while I jerked off, but it felt good. Really good. But her reaction was... cruel. Way more than it ever needed to be. She said horrible and hateful things to me, and it made it clear how little room there was for my desires in that relationship if they didn't align with hers. Long story short, asking her to fuck me was the start of the end. She couldn't get over it, and she ultimately held it over me, making me feel worse and worse with every interaction we had. I was already nervous about sharing that part of myself with someone else, about admitting how I truly felt, so her continued reaction made me question if she was right—if there was something wrong with me. And we divorced shortly after."

"I'm so sorry, baby," I murmur. "That's awful. But I'm really fucking glad you got out of a marriage with someone who made you feel that way about yourself, and that we found each other, because you never have to hide what you want here. We'll explore all of it together, safely. I'll never judge you for what turns you on."

He lets out a deep breath, sinking further into me as he wraps his arms around mine over his chest.

"Before, sex never felt like it does with you. Even though it's been hard on Sam, and single-parenting isn't a walk in the park, her walking out of our lives is the best thing that's happened to me. Well, besides meeting you," he admits, and I give his red cheek a quick kiss. "I didn't realize how trapped I felt in that marriage. I had just accepted that was my life, and there'd always be a quiet part of me that wondered what it would be like to be with a man."

I press a kiss to the side of his neck. "I understand that. I'm sorry it was so hard. You don't have to carry any of that alone anymore."

"Nash?" Caleb asks hesitantly.

"Hmm?"

"Can you…" he starts, voice a little shy. "Can you put your dick in me and just let me sit on you? While we're in here? It's something I've always wanted to try."

My heart swells at how softly he asks. "Yeah, baby. Of course I can. You should still have my cum and some lube in you since we haven't washed you yet, so I should sink right in. Just one second."

He shifts, and I stroke myself to get hard enough to slide

into him easily. Once I'm there, I help him shift forward and sit up slightly to position himself over me. When he sinks down onto my cock, we both let out quiet, broken breaths.

His back presses against my chest again, and I hold him tighter than before, our bodies joined together. His fingers slide along my thighs, and mine rest over his heart. His body relaxes a little more, chest rising and falling in a slower rhythm.

"Is there anything else you want to explore together?" I ask, voice low against his ear. He's so warm and tight, but I don't want to make this about sex when I know it's about comfort for him. "How are you feeling after tonight?"

"So much better now that you're back inside of me." He laughs softly. "I like the feeling of being used by you, like I'm nothing more than a hole for your pleasure. But I also love the praise mixed with the degradation. It lets me experience and give in to my desires without feeling self-conscious because I'm doing exactly what you're telling me."

"Mmmm," I hum. "It turns me on too. All of it. And you're so much more than a hole to me, even if that's how you want me to treat you during sex."

"I know." He swallows. "I bought the dildo after she and I separated because I was always jealous of the bottom in the porn I was watching. Turns out, I had every right to be jealous."

"I love filling you up the way you crave," I murmur, sliding my hand down his back. "I do want to check, though. Do you ever want to top me?"

He shifts against me as he thinks and lets out a small sigh. "Not really. I mean… if it's something you wanted, I'd be open to trying, of course. But what we've been doing feels good. I like handing control over to you and bottoming, a lot.

More than I even thought I would. But if you want me to, I will."

I press a kiss to his temple and let my hand settle over his hip.

"Nope," I say softly. "That's all I needed to hear."

"How did you know you were attracted to men?" he asks, and I don't think anyone's ever asked me before.

"That's a hard question because there isn't a specific time that comes to mind for me," I start. "I never had a 'this is it' moment. It never felt like I was fighting anything when I was dating women. I noticed guys, but didn't pursue them, and when I had the opportunity to hook up with my friend from class after we'd been drinking, I jumped on it. That's what solidified it for me."

"Did anyone in your life care?" he asks as he shifts on my lap with another little groan.

I swallow, wanting to be honest with him without rubbing it in. "When I told my family, I was met with support, thankfully. Have you ever told yours?"

"No, we don't really talk as it is, and that would be the final straw. I've accepted that, and I already went through enough shame with my ex, I don't need to go through it with my parents too..." he trails off. "Though... I think she might've told them I'm gay or something since they've been even more distant since the divorce. Or maybe it's just the fact that I got divorced. I never asked since it doesn't matter. I don't want to subject Sam to that kind of conditional love." He sighs.

"I'm so proud of you for doing what's best for you and Sam. But Cay, please hear me when I say this... their reaction is a *them* problem, not a *you* problem. There is nothing shameful about who you are, and you don't have to keep carrying their shame. But you have to decide when you're done holding it."

He's quiet for a few moments before sighing. "You're right," he says.

I tighten my arms around him, rubbing his thighs and pressing kisses along his neck and shoulders.

We sit like that for a few minutes, until he starts shifting more, rubbing his ass against my thighs, and I notice his dick getting hard again. Gently, I wrap my hand around him, stroking slowly to comfort him the way he's always deserved to be cared for.

He leans his head back against my shoulder, breath catching slightly. He moans as I stroke him and continue kissing him, and in this silence, I know without question that I'd do anything to make him feel safe like this.

CHAPTER 23
Caleb

"No missed calls or texts from Tess, so I assume that means she made it through the night fine with all three kids," Nash says as he rolls over to check his phone, his voice still scratchy with sleep.

It's terrifying to let your kid go anywhere for the night, period. But letting him stay with your boyfriend's ex-wife who you've only met once, who you're trusting not just with bedtime, but with your whole heart wrapped up in a third grader's body? That's next-level vulnerability.

Last night, I thought I'd be a wreck. I thought I'd lie awake obsessively checking my phone, worried sick about him. But between the party, the drinks, and Nash making me come twice with his hands on me and his cock in me, I was too worn out to be stressed.

Sam has a basic phone without internet, so he knows how to reach me if he needs anything. Since I hadn't heard from him last night, I text him while we're still in bed.

> You doing okay, bud? How was your night?

I watch the screen for a minute, waiting until he texts back.

SAM:

> It was so fun! I want to have more sleepovers!

I let out a breath and laugh softly. "Well, that answers that question."

Nash turns toward me, one arm tucked behind his head. "Good news?"

"Sam says he wants to have more sleepovers. I guess Tess survived, and he had fun."

"Didn't doubt her." He grins and pulls me back into him in bed. "Told you it'd be okay. She's a great mom."

I nuzzle into him a little, letting the tension I hadn't even realized I was holding bleed out of me. "Alright. Now that I'm feeling better, we can order room service."

He kisses the side of my head. "Good. You earned breakfast in bed, baby. You were incredible last night."

I smile at his praise as he grabs the menu from the desk in the room. We look through it, settling on coffee and the classic breakfast with eggs, toast, hash browns, and bacon.

Nash calls while I slide back against the pillows. He orders, murmurs confirmations, and then hangs up, pulling me closer to him.

The next thing I register is a knock at the door and the sound of Nash's bare feet hitting the floor.

"Room service!" someone calls brightly from the hall.

Nash grabs a pair of sweatpants from his bag, pulling them up over his hips. He opens the door, his bare back to me. He takes the food and thanks the person.

"Sir, your feast has arrived," he announces, that familiar

cocky grin tugging at his lips as he turns and rolls the cart into the room.

I sit up, laughing. "Thank you kindly."

He climbs back into bed, placing the tray of food in front of us. He reaches for a slice of bacon, still shirtless, and smirks at me with his bedhead and stupidly kissable mouth. When he's done chewing, he pours our coffees in the white porcelain hotel mugs while I start to eat.

"So..." I break the silence after a few bites. "Did I pass the boyfriend-at-a-work-party test?"

Nash looks up from his coffee with a mock-serious expression. "You did more than pass. You're hired for the gig full-time if you'd like it," he says, then cracks a grin.

"Benefits include...?"

"Unlimited snuggles. Occasional hotel stays. Complimentary kids' sleepovers, schedule permitting. And a boyfriend who fucks you just how you like, every time."

"That's a pretty solid package," I say, leaning back against the headboard. "Hmm, tempting."

"Unless you have other offers."

I shake my head. "Not a one."

He laughs, pulling me forward into a quick kiss.

"I accept, of course." I grin.

No part of me understands how I got this lucky with Nash. He's kind and caring, and everything I've dreamed of—both in bed and in the rest of my life.

I'm all in with him.

We eat the last bites of breakfast, and he shows me a photo Tess just sent him of the kids building a blanket fort in the living room. Sam's face is lit up with joy, and my chest aches with how much I miss him.

"It looks like they had a great time," I say, smiling.

"It sure does." Nash taps the screen, saving the photo before setting the phone down. "Ready to head out and go see them?"

"Yeah. It's only been a night, but I miss him."

"I understand that. Let's shower quickly before we head out."

I nod, and Nash goes into the bathroom, turning the water on before I join him.

We step in, and the warmth hits me instantly. I let the water wash over my face and shoulders, feeling the tinge of soreness in my thighs and back from my position last night. Nash reaches for my waist, pulling me back against his chest as his lips brush the curve of my neck.

"Sore?" he asks.

"Little bit," I admit with a quiet laugh. "But it's a good sore."

"Yeah?" He noses behind my ear. "What about here?" His hands slide down to my hips, his fingers grazing the inside of my thighs until they grip my dick. "Still needy?"

I bite my lip and nod, leaning my head back against his shoulder. "Always needy for you."

"Want me to make you come one more time before we go home?"

I groan, because I do. Of course I do. I always want Nash's hands on me.

"Yes, touch me."

Nash pours some body wash into his palm, rubs it between his hands until it's slick and warm, then presses a kiss to the back of my neck. "Turn around."

I do, and he pulls me in until our chests are nearly touching. He nudges one foot between mine to make more space, and then his hand wraps around both of our cocks.

The sensation is immediate. Hot, tight, perfect. I groan, bracing myself with one hand on his shoulder, the other against the slippery tile beside us as he strokes us together in his strong, steady grip.

"Feel good?" he asks.

"Fuck, Nash," I breathe, already thrusting into his fist, chasing the friction. "So good."

He leans in, mouth skimming my jaw, his free hand gripping my hip to keep me close. "I love watching you fall apart for me, baby. You're so fucking pretty when you come."

I'm so close already, I'm shaking as the water continues pounding around us. Our skin is slick and hot, sliding together in a perfect rhythm.

"Nash. Gonna come," I grit out, seconds before I finally let go. My hips jerk forward, chasing his hand, and a strangled sound tears from my throat as I spill across his hand and stomach.

Nash doesn't stop. He keeps going until he's groaning too, forehead pressed to mine, coming with a low, broken sound that sends another ripple of heat down my spine.

He captures my mouth mid-groan, and it's such a messy, depraved kiss with so much tongue. It's everything. The definition of passion.

"You good?" he checks after he pulls away and catches his breath.

"Yeah," I say, blinking up at him with a dazed smile. "I think you just scrambled my brain. That was amazing."

"Good." He laughs and kisses me quicker this time. "Let's rinse off. Then we can get out of here."

We finish the shower, then a few minutes later, we're dressed, packed up, and ready to head to the kids.

By the time we're in the car, I'm clean, warm, and still

carrying the buzz of being wanted so thoroughly. Nash keeps one hand on the wheel and the other on my thigh as we drive toward Tess's neighborhood. His thumb rubs slow, absent circles against my jeans.

It's everything I could have ever wanted.

"Hey, Cay?" he says, glancing at me briefly before looking back at the road.

"Yeah?" I turn slightly in my seat.

"I was thinking…" He pauses. "I'd really enjoy doing Christmas with you and Sam. What do you think about that?"

My chest tightens in the best kind of way. I wasn't sure if we were there yet; we've only known each other for a few weeks, but somehow it just feels right. Everything about him and us feels right.

"I'd love to," I say, meaning every word. "Are you sure?"

"Very sure," he says, giving my thigh a squeeze. "I want this to be real. I want the tree, the chaos of opening presents, the matching pajamas with the kids—if you'll humor me—the whole thing."

A soft laugh escapes me. "I can't think of anything I'd enjoy more. I haven't done a holiday like that in a long time."

"Then we'll start new traditions," Nash says easily. "I'll talk to Tess today—see what the schedule looks like and how we can make it work."

"Okay," I agree, voice a little thick. "Thank you for asking."

"Thank you for saying yes."

CHAPTER 24

Nash

Christmas is only four days away now, and somehow, everything feels a little more romantic and cozy because of it.

The moment we find a spot to park on the street, Benji throws the back door open, and he and Sam are scrambling out of the car to wait on the sidewalk. Emma unbuckles herself, and I open her door so she can hop out as Caleb opens the trunk to grab the gloves and scarves we packed.

We meet the boys and head to the downtown rink. It's alive in only the way December can bring with holiday classics flowing through the speakers above the ice. The music is just loud enough to compete with the slicing of blades on the ice and the laughter of families and couples skating around the pop-up rink.

Emma tugs on my hand as we walk up to the counter to pay and get our rentals.

"Dad, do you think I'll fall?" she asks, her voice a jittery mix of nerves and excitement.

I crouch down in front of her. "Nope. Last year's skills will come right back. Just like skiing."

"Promise?"

"Yep, and I'll be right there if you need to get your legs under you first. You can hold my hand while we get started."

She smiles and seems satisfied enough with my answer to go back to talking with the boys. After we're all fitted for our skates and paid up, Caleb helps Sam put on his skates, and I help Benji and Emma. When it's our turn, we sit beside each other on the bench, and I can feel the cold from the metal bench seeping through my clothes. Not sure who thought of making outdoor benches metal, but it's uncomfortable. Caleb's thigh presses against mine, though, as he bends forward to tie his laces, and it gives me a subtle kind of warmth.

"Think we'll survive this?" he asks under his breath as he ties his second lace.

"We got all three here in one piece. That's already a win."

We both laugh, standing up, ready to head toward the ice. Emma pulls on my hand toward the entrance. Sam and Benji are walking in front of us, unaware of the other people around us, so I place my hand on Benji's shoulder to steer him clear of an incoming group that he pays no attention to.

Once we're on the ice, Emma keeps her hand in mine, but she also reaches for Caleb's hand. "Can we all skate together?" she asks, and my heart melts despite the cold we're surrounded by.

"Of course we can," Caleb responds.

I smile at him, loving how incredible he is with my daughter.

Emma sticks close to us for a few laps until her confidence builds, and then she's off, skating ahead, trying to keep up with the boys like she always does. Her laugh echoes off the ice, and the snow lightly falling around us makes everything feel like we're on a movie set.

Now that my hand is free, I glance at Caleb. I want to reach for him, but we haven't spoken to the kids yet.

Caleb bumps his shoulder gently into mine. "This is nice, huh?"

"Couldn't be more perfect. Especially with the snow." I pause, then add under my breath, "Unless I was able to hold your hand."

He glances sideways at me with a half smile before steadying himself. "Uh, should we... talk to them soon? No pressure if you're not there yet, but I think I am."

I nod, watching as Benji loops past us, skating backwards. "I'd love to have that conversation. Besides, they're smart, so I think they kind of sense it. Emma asked me the other day if we were friends who like each other," I admit with a laugh.

Caleb winces. "Okay. So... maybe it's time?"

"Tonight? Tomorrow?" I ask. It sounds soon, and I don't want to push if it feels like too much, but I also really want them to know. I want to be able to hold his hand and kiss him, and show everyone how much I adore the man by my side.

He watches Sam try to spin and nearly wipe out before nodding slowly. "Yeah. What if I talk to Sam tonight when we get home? He already wants to sleep over at your house tonight. Maybe we both could?"

I love that we're making this plan together. Caleb's used to carrying everything himself and making every decision on his own. And now, he's asking me, letting me shoulder a piece of it.

"I think that's a great plan, baby," I say softly, eyes

following the kids as they skate past, cheeks flushed from the cold. "And I think it'll feel better once we tell them."

"Me too."

I glance over, knowing how big of a deal this is for him. "Is there anything you're worried about with Sam?"

Caleb sighs and bites his lip. "It's not one specific thing. He's a good kid, he likes you, and he loves being with Benji and Emma. I don't think he'll be upset, but…" He pauses, and my stomach sinks just a little at his hesitation. "It's just been the two of us since his mom left."

I nod, listening and understanding where he's coming from.

"And now this is… different," he says. "You're different. What we have feels different, and it might be crazy to say this, but it feels lasting. I want him to know what we have, and I want to grow our life together. But I also don't want him to feel like anything's changing in a way that might leave him out."

"He won't," I promise him gently. "You've built a world where he knows he comes first. That won't go away, and I think this is going to make his world bigger—not smaller—because it feels real to me too. I want it all with you, Cay, or I wouldn't be suggesting we have this conversation with the kids."

Caleb's lips twitch like he's trying not to smile, but it wins anyway. "You're really good at saying exactly what I need to hear, you know that?"

"Guess I'm just a softie for a guy with a cute kid who turned out to be best friends with mine." I grin, nudging him.

"Thank you," he says, looking up at me through his lashes as snowflakes fall on his beautiful face. I want to kiss him so badly.

"Can we get hot cocoa now?" Benji skates up to me, tugging on my coat.

"Please, Dad," Emma adds dramatically, and I laugh because it's always something.

"Hot cocoa sounds perfect," Caleb says, grinning over his shoulder at me, so hot cocoa it is.

We help the kids off the ice, trade skates for boots, and head toward the pop-up holiday market just past the park. Vendors have their tents up, selling everything from hand-made candles and wool scarves to pastries and ornaments. Holiday music continues to play from speakers somewhere, and snow flurries drift down like confetti.

"Okay," I say, adjusting Emma's hat over her ears, "who wants cocoa?"

"Me!" all three kids yell at once.

Caleb laughs beside me, and we all head to stand in line. The line moves quickly, and once everyone has their cocoa in hand, we walk through the booths. The kids aren't all that excited to be shopping, but at least they have their drink.

We duck into a booth to admire the hand-painted ornaments they have on display.

"This one's silly," Emma says, giggling. It's a snowman holding a sled mid-slip.

"You like it?" I ask, crouching beside her.

She nods. "He looks like he's gonna fall."

"I think that's part of the charm." I glance up at Caleb and catch him smiling at us, watching the interaction, eyes crinkled at the corners.

An idea sparks, and I turn toward him. "Hey… what do you say we pick out an ornament together? One that's ours, and we can hang it on the tree we cut down together. First of many, hopefully. It can turn into our little tradition."

"I really like that idea," he says, reaching to squeeze my hand quickly where the kids can't see.

Benji appears next to us with Sam in tow. "They have a snowboarding moose over there," he says. "It's so cool!"

Sam pipes up, as usual, always building on Benji's ideas. "Please, Dad. The moose is so cool!"

Emma, still holding her snowman, looks up. "Can we pick one for all of us?"

"Sure," Caleb agrees. "I think I know what I'm getting for us," he says, turning to me.

Caleb ends up buying both the snowman and the moose wearing goggles with a snowboard tucked under its furry arm. He also picks out a cabin ornament for us that's covered in snow and a perfect representation of our first weekend together after unexpectedly being snowed in together.

"These guys are going front and center on the tree, aren't they?" I ask as we walk back toward the park bench.

"Absolutely," Caleb confirms.

CHAPTER 25

Caleb

Sam wants to stay the night with Benji, but I know I need to have this conversation first.

"Hey, bud," I say. "Let's stop home first before you head to Benji's so we can get some clothes. I also want to talk to you for a few minutes."

He groans dramatically. "Why?"

"I just need to talk to you first, one-on-one. Won't take long. Promise."

He eyes me warily, clearly suspicious now. "Am I in trouble?"

"Nope," I say, brushing off his shoulders from the snow. "Not at all."

He shrugs and agrees, probably because he's used to listening to me. But I know that won't last forever. He's eight now, and tonight, I'm going to ask him to make room for someone else in our life. Or three more someones, technically. I think he'll be excited, but I'm unsure at the same time.

We pile back in the car, and Nash drops us off at our house.

"Thanks, Nash. I'll text you when I'm done talking and hopefully heading back over."

"Okay," he says back. "And hey, Cay? You got this."

It's another moment I deeply wish I could lean forward and kiss him. *Soon*, I remind myself. That's the point of this entire conversation I'm nervous as hell to have with my son.

Inside, Sam toes off his boots and hangs up his jacket, then plops onto the couch. He pulls the blanket off the back, and I turn on the gas fireplace in the center of the room before sitting on the other end of the couch.

He looks over at me. "What is it, Dad?"

I smile gently. "You know how we've been spending more time with Nash and the kids lately?"

"Yeah," he says quickly. "It's fun. I like Benji. And Emma's funny."

I nod. "They really like you too. And I think you've probably noticed that I like being around Nash."

Sam blinks at me for a moment. "Like… as a friend?"

Here goes nothing.

"Well, more than that. Nash and I have been spending time together because we really like each other in the way some grown-ups do."

He frowns slightly, like he's thinking through something bigger than the words.

"Like you used to like Mom?" he asks without accusation, more so confusion.

"Yes. Your mom is great because she gave me you." I say that because it's true, and I never bad-mouth his mom in front of him. "But sometimes feelings change as you grow, and sometimes you learn new things about yourself too. And for me, that meant realizing I could like Nash."

He looks down at his fingers in his lap, quiet for a second. "So you like boys and girls?"

"Yeah, I do," I say. But even as I say it, there's a flicker of doubt. Because lately, I've been wondering if I'm actually gay, not bi.

I haven't said that part out loud yet. It's just been one of those quiet thoughts hanging out in my mind.

With women, I think I tried so hard to make it feel right because that's what I was supposed to want. I thought that's what I did want. But now, being with Nash has made everything feel different. I'm not sure how to unravel years of assumptions and expectations. Unsure how to tell what was genuine attraction versus emotional safety or pressure or performative closeness because I loved my ex, once upon a time, I really did.

I'm not ashamed of being bi, if that's what I am, but I've started questioning if that's the right label for me the more time I spend with Nash.

Everything with him just feels better. Still, I don't want to make Sam attempt to sort something I haven't even figured out myself.

It's hard living in a world that clings to labels so much. It adds a layer of pressure, even if Nash has never asked me to define my sexuality.

So instead, I just smile.

"And," I continue, "I like Nash a lot, and it's important to me that you know how I feel about him because you're the most important person in my life, and I want you to feel included."

He nods slowly. "Okay… I guess that makes sense." Then after a moment, he grins. "Does this mean more sleepovers with Benji?"

"Only if you're comfortable. You'd still have your space, Sam. Nothing about us changes."

He's quiet again, then says, "I want more sleepovers. It's like I'll have a brother and a sister now! Right?"

"You can definitely see them more, yes," I half-answer. "Thank you for being open."

He nods. "Can we go now? We were gonna do two layers of pillows this time in the fort."

"Yeah." I chuckle. "Go get your stuff" barely leaves my mouth before Sam disappears down the hallway to pack a bag.

I sit on the couch for another second, the weight of the conversation slowly lifting off my chest. Our talk went exactly how I'd hoped it'd go, and while Sam will probably have more questions when he's not so focused on going over there, he seemed okay with it, and that's all that matters.

I grab my phone and text Nash.

> Talked to Sam and it went well. He's pumped about more sleepovers.

NASH:

> I knew it'd go great. You still going to come over?

I glance toward the hallway, where I can hear Sam slamming his dresser drawers.

> Yes, let me go get a bag packed. How did it go with Benji and Emma?

NASH:

> They couldn't be more excited either, baby.

I toss my phone onto the bed and grab my overnight bag

from the closet, throwing in a change of clothes, a toothbrush, and a phone charger. I pause when I get to my dresser, eyes lingering on the framed photo of Sam and me at the lake last summer. He's holding a fish, and I'm squinting into the sun behind him, proud as hell. I can almost imagine a new photo of the five of us in that exact spot with even bigger smiles and so much more love.

"Hey, buddy?" I call down the hall as I zip my bag. "You ready?"

"Yes!"

By the time we're in the car, I'm aware I should give Sam the heads-up that I'll be staying too.

"Hey," I say, glancing over as I back out of the driveway. "Just so you know, I'm planning to hang out with Nash tonight. I might sleep over there too."

He looks up from where he's fiddling with the zipper on his coat. "Oh. Cool. So like… a double sleepover?"

I smile. "Pretty much."

"Okay," he says with a shrug. "Can we have cinnamon rolls in the morning?"

"Yeah, I'm sure we can make that happen." I laugh.

As we pull up to Nash's place, the porch lights cast a soft golden glow over the snow-covered steps. Twinkling lights wrap around the railing and line his roof, and a wreath hangs on the front door, framed by a few simple fake Christmas trees on both sides. It's cozy, festive, and homey.

The second we park, Sam's already unbuckling. He grabs his backpack and bolts up the steps, full of energy, and knocks on the door.

Nash opens the door, already smiling. "Hey, you made it."

"Hi! Yep!" Sam says, barging right in and kicking off his shoes.

"We did," I chuckle at Sam's enthusiasm as he runs toward Benji and Emma in the living room.

Nash leans in slightly, voice low enough that only I can hear. "You okay?"

I nod, more than okay. "Yes, and even better now."

"Mmm, me too." He brushes his hand lightly against mine in that small, just-us way. "Come on in."

"So"—I grin, unzipping my coat—"Sam's fine with me staying tonight, but I did promise him cinnamon rolls in the morning to seal the deal. What are the chances you've got some in the fridge?"

"Approximately zero." Nash laughs, and so do I.

"No big deal," I say, setting my bag near the bench by the door. "I was planning to order some to be delivered tonight or in the morning anyway."

"Or"—Nash holds up a finger—"we could make them from scratch. Or at least attempt. I've got tons of baking stuff in the kitchen, and it could be a lot of fun."

We walk toward the kitchen together while the kids play in the living room. Warmth seeps into my chest as I'm finally stepping into the version of my life I didn't even know I was waiting for. I've never once had the impulse to make cinnamon rolls from scratch, but suddenly, nothing sounds better.

I look around his kitchen. It's clean but lived-in with a couple of scribbled grocery reminders stuck to the fridge and the kids' hand-drawn art. He's got wood cabinets and granite countertops.

"Okay, Chef Nash," I tease, bringing my eyes back to him. "What do we need to make these cinnamon rolls?"

"No idea." He laughs. "That's what the internet is for."

I'm grinning from ear to ear because doing this with him

makes everything feel lighter and better. Almost like home is something we're building together in real time.

While he pulls up a recipe, I stand here admiring him until he starts listing ingredients and telling me where to find them.

"Before we get started, let me get the resident playlist curator." Nash smirks, calling for Emma.

"Yeah, Dad?" she asks with rosy cheeks.

"Will you put on a Christmas playlist for us to make these cinnamon rolls for you guys?"

"Yes!" she shouts, telling Alexa to play her favorite station.

"Now we can begin," Nash declares, and Emma runs back into the living room.

We start by warming the milk and butter on the stove, and Nash dips his pinky into the pot. "Warm, but not boiling hot," he declares. "Good enough, I suppose."

I nod. "If it's good for you, it's good for me."

He whisks in the yeast while I mix the dry ingredients, then we combine them all into the mixer bowl, and the dough starts to come together slowly.

By the time we roll out the dough, we're both covered in flour, and I don't think I'd ever volunteer to make cinnamon rolls from scratch again... well, unless Nash wanted to.

Once they're ready to sit in the fridge overnight, we clean up the absolute explosion we've left behind with dishes in the sink, flour on the floor, and sugar on the top of the stove.

Nash wipes his hands on a towel and looks over at me like he's about to say something serious. Instead, he just says, "That was fun."

"You're fun," I say before I can stop myself, and when he looks over at me, his eyes are soft. He steps closer, hands resting lightly on my waist, like he's not sure if he should lean in yet.

"I'm gonna kiss you now," he declares.

"Okay," I whisper.

And he does.

It's sweet, unhurried, and tastes like cinnamon.

It's my new favorite flavor.

CHAPTER 26
Nash

T he smell of cinnamon hits me before I even open my eyes. I shift in bed, reaching out, but the space next to me is empty, and the sheets are cold. I hear movement down the hall, followed by laughter, and it all comes back to me.

Caleb staying the night with the kids knowing, and us making homemade cinnamon rolls before bed. And apparently, he let me sleep in this morning while he wrangled the children, which is a major luxury and deserving of another brutal fucking, like I know he craves.

I wish we'd gotten to wake up like we did at the hotel, but knowing he came down my throat last night is still satisfying, even if I didn't get to fuck him against a window wall for all of Denver to see.

There's more laughter coming from the kitchen, and I really don't want to miss these moments, so I roll out of bed, go to the bathroom, and quickly get dressed.

When I walk into the kitchen, the cinnamon rolls are already on the table, still warm and freshly iced, and slightly lopsided in a way that makes me love them more. Benji is mid-bite with icing on his face, and Emma's eyes widen with pure joy when she sees me, cinnamon roll in hand. Sam's the only civilized-looking one eating his with a fork. *Leave it to my kids.*

Caleb glances up from where he's pouring coffee. "Morning."

"Morning." I rub a hand across my face and head straight for the coffee, bumping my shoulder against his. "They turned out okay?"

Emma answers before Caleb can. "They're so good, Dad. Can you make them more?"

I lean in and press a quick kiss to Caleb's cheek without really thinking about it—just one of those small, sleepy morning things that I've been wanting to do since we met.

But the second I pull back, one of the kids gasps as the house falls silent.

Benji, Emma, and I had a quick talk last night, and they seemed totally fine when I told them I liked Caleb and hoped he and Sam would be around more, but I'm realizing right now that maybe I didn't spell it out clearly enough.

The kids are looking at us expectantly as I quickly glance at Caleb, but Emma speaks first.

"Wait. You guys kiss now?"

Caleb clears his throat, clearly trying to keep a straight face. "That was a kiss on the cheek."

"Still counts," Benji says, wiping his mouth. "That's definitely a dating thing."

Sam shrugs. "I already knew."

Benji whips his head toward him. "What?"

"Dad told me last night. I think it's cool," Sam says. "Besides, we get cinnamon rolls."

"We get cinnamon rolls because they're dating?" Benji asks, clearly confused by Sam's logic.

"Yeah, I think. Dad told me last night he liked your dad, and then I asked for cinnamon rolls when he said he was going to sleep over too. Would you rather not get cinnamon rolls?" Sam replies, and I want to laugh at kid logic, but this is a big moment for all of us.

Emma looks between us with a questioning look. "So… you guys are boyfriends? You kiss?"

Caleb and I both nod. "Yeah," I say gently. "We are."

"We wanted to make sure we talked to all of you," Caleb adds, his voice warm. "We care what you think, since this affects you too, and we want to make sure everyone feels okay about it."

Emma nods along as Caleb speaks. "What about Christmas?"

Part of me wants to laugh because, of course, that's what she leads with. Not the kissing or us being boyfriends. Christmas.

Caleb glances at me, and I reach for his hand, giving it a quick squeeze.

"We still have to talk about that," I say carefully, glancing at all three kids. "But I'd love for us to celebrate with Caleb and Sam… if you're all okay with it."

Emma reaches for another cinnamon roll and says, through a mouthful of frosting, "So does that mean Sam is our brother now?"

"Are we all gonna live together?" Benji adds, looking back and forth between us. "Like, in one big house?"

Caleb's eyes widen slightly, and I have to fight a laugh. Not at the question, but at how fast kids can go from do we kiss to a new blended family home in under ten seconds.

"Okay, so… no one's moving in anywhere just yet," I say, trying to keep my tone light but honest. "But those are big questions, and they're important, so if that is something we were thinking about, we'd talk to you all first so you could be part of that conversation."

Caleb nods beside me. "What matters most right now is that everyone feels safe and loved and valued. That's what we care about."

"I think it sounds kinda fun," Sam pipes up. "Even if we don't get to move to a big house."

He glances at Emma and Benji, and Benji grins in return.

"Me too," Benji says, nudging Sam's arm. Emma nods quickly beside them, wiping cinnamon from her hands onto her pajama pants, and I groan, moving to give her a napkin.

"Emma." I sigh, reaching for a napkin. "We have so many napkins, honey."

She blinks up at me and shrugs, taking the napkin from my hand as I let out a laugh. The tension in the room loosens a little, and I know there'll be more questions eventually, but for now, I think we're good.

I glance around the table. "Do you guys want to hang your new ornaments on the tree after breakfast?"

Three little voices answer at once.

"Yes!"

CHAPTER 27
Caleb

Sam's curled up on the couch with a throw blanket around his shoulders, half-heartedly watching *Home Alone*. He's been quiet since dinner, and I know that look. It's the same one I've seen after his mom forgets to call on his birthday.

"You okay, buddy?" I ask, sitting beside him.

He shrugs. "I just thought today would be more fun. It's Christmas Eve."

"I know," I say gently. "I miss Benji and Emma too."

He leans his head on my arm and sighs. He hated learning they'd be with their mom tonight, and I know the more our relationship progresses, it'll always be hard for him the nights they're gone.

I glance at the clock, hoping I can fix this even slightly.

"Hey," I say, grabbing my phone. "Do you want Nash to come over? Would that be more fun? We could do our own Christmas Eve stuff. We could bake something, if you want. Or play a game."

Sam lifts his head. "Yeah. Can we play Uno?"

I smile. "We can definitely play Uno."

> Any chance you're free? Sam's missing
> your kids and I'm missing you.

He replies instantly.

NASH:

> Me too. I'll bring cookie dough. See you in
> 20 mins, baby.

"Alright, Nash is coming, and he said he'd bring cookie dough."

Sam's face lights up, and I'm relieved he's excited. "Awesome! I hope it's chocolate chip."

I ruffle Sam's hair as I stand. "Let me turn on the fire. You can go clear the table so we're ready for a cookie-and-card battle when he gets here."

Sam's already tossing his blanket aside and racing to the kitchen drawer where we keep the cards. I head to the fireplace, flipping the switch to ignite the gas logs, and the room instantly feels warmer—not just from the heat, but from the shift in mood.

By the time Nash knocks at the front door, I feel like I can breathe again.

It's not that anything's wrong—Sam and I have always had a good time on our own. We've built a life that works for just the two of us. One that I'm proud of. But ever since Nash and his kids stepped into our world, something inside me shifted, and I think Sam feels it too. Nash didn't just fit into our world; he brought something with him that made it bigger and somehow better.

There's something grounding about having him here for both of us, because the moment Sam sees Nash standing in the doorway, his face lights up. For the first time in a long time, we both have someone else we can lean on. Someone who gives us more than they take and makes us feel important.

Nash makes me realize I'm allowed to dream past the walls I'd built around our lives, and it feels like that extra space is what we both needed.

"Merry Christmas Eve," Nash says cheerfully as he steps inside.

"Hi, Nash!" Sam grins, running over. "Did you bring chocolate chip cookie dough?"

"Chocolate chip *and* sugar cookie," Nash confirms. "Thought we could get creative."

"Awesome!" Sam beams before turning around and heading back into the kitchen. "Come on, I'll get the pan out!"

We both chuckle at his enthusiasm, but I can't ignore the sense of relief and peace I feel knowing the positive effect Nash has on Sam.

Nash leans forward to give me a quick kiss. "You okay?"

"Yeah," I murmur. "He's so much happier you're here, and so am I."

He reaches for my hand, interlocking our fingers, and kisses me again before pulling back. "Me too. I'm so excited we get to spend Christmas Eve together. Now, come on, before we keep Sam waiting any longer."

We walk hand in hand into the kitchen. Sam's already got the trays spread out, and Nash sets the dough on the counter while I turn on the oven. We pull apart the cookie dough piece by piece to line the baking tray and pop them in the oven.

"I went easy on you this time with the premade cookie dough," Nash says as he nudges me with his arm.

"After the cinnamon rolls, thank god for that." I play

along, but truthfully, I'd make anything he asked for from scratch.

"Alright, timer is set," Nash confirms as he pops the tray of cookies into the oven.

"Let's play Uno while we wait!" Sam exclaims. He's got the deck ready to go on the table. Sam deals and makes sure we know the rules. "Stacking +2 cards is allowed."

"You're a monster," Nash says, pretending to gasp.

"I learned from the best," Sam shoots back, looking at me, and I'm smiling so hard my face actually hurts. This isn't how I imagined Christmas Eve going, but it's already better than all our other Christmas Eves.

After we eat the cookies and play multiple rounds of Uno, Sam finally starts to yawn between turns.

"Ready for bed?" I ask him, assuming he'll ask to stay up a little longer.

"Yes!" He turns to rush off toward his bedroom. "Santa's coming!"

I chuckle as I get up to follow him, and Nash surprises me by coming with me.

"No reason for you to do bedtime by yourself while I'm here," he assures me, and knowing he wants to help makes my chest ache.

"Thanks, Nash."

After Sam brushes his teeth and changes into his pajamas, I lay next to Sam in bed while Nash sits on the foot of the bed.

"I pulled out our signature Christmas Eve book earlier," I tell Nash, holding it up.

"*The Night Before Christmas*!" Sam adds excitedly.

"That's a good one," Nash says, smiling at me as I begin

to read to Sam until he drifts off. We sneak out of his room, shutting Sam's bedroom door behind us.

"Do you want to be Santa now or later?" I ask Nash.

"Hmm, I vote later, because there's something else I'd rather do with you right now," he says, pulling me in the direction of my room.

I smile, and there are so many emotions running through me. I can't believe I'm finally getting to experience a Christmas with someone I love… because I do love him. The realization makes me pause. It's only been weeks, and yet my life is undeniably better with him in it. I feel fuller, and happier, and safer. I trust Nash, and I'm so excited for our future together.

When we get inside, he turns toward me. "You always get this quiet at night or is something wrong, baby?"

I let out a quiet laugh and try to sum up what I'm feeling. "No, nothing's wrong. Just… before you came, Sam was quiet, and I could tell he was sad. But the second you walked in, he lit up. And watching how easy it is for him to be happy around you made me realize just how much you already mean to us. Both of us."

Nash leans in and presses a kiss to my temple. "That makes me really happy to hear. I got lucky with you both."

My throat tightens. I want to tell him we're the lucky ones, but before I can say anything, he kisses me. His warm lips meet mine like he's trying to tell me he's got me, that he's here because he wants to be, not because I asked.

My hand curls around the back of his neck, holding him there, needing to feel him as close as possible as his tongue glides against mine. My stomach flips as he guides me toward the bed until I fall backwards. He climbs on top of me, grinding down on me. My hips tilt instinctively toward the weight of him.

The kiss deepens as his hand slips under my shirt, fingers warm against my skin, and I swear my whole chest cracks open under the weight of how much I want this—him.

When he finally pulls back, he rests his forehead against mine, and I feel his breath fan across my lips.

"Do you want me to blow you?"

"Yes," I breathe. I don't even hesitate because I'll always want more of him. Always.

He stands quickly and begins undressing, and I follow suit—my eyes tracing every inch of his gorgeous, toned body. I can't help licking my lips as he pushes his underwear down, revealing a trail of dark hair that leads right to his hard, waiting cock.

Nash climbs back on top of me, fully naked now. The second his hand cradles my jaw, I melt into his touch, into the kiss that deepens between us. His tongue nudges at the seam of my mouth, and I open for him easily again. Then he shifts, rolling over me, his hips pressing down.

"Mmm," he murmurs against my lips, his hips continuing to grind slowly against mine. "So hard for me already."

He bites down on my lip, and I whimper before he licks it and shoves his tongue back into my mouth. Him treating me like he can do anything to me is unbelievably hot, and I can't get enough of it.

Nash's hand slides under my ass, giving it a squeeze, and just the pressure of his palm has my hips thrusting for more of anything he's willing to give me.

"Does your cock need attention, Cay?"

I nod. "Please."

"Say it, baby."

"Fuck, Nash… Please touch me. I need you."

He leans in to kiss me again before he shifts lower. His mouth brushes over my jaw, then my throat, his breath hot against my skin. My chest arches when he sucks one of my nipples into his mouth and bites just enough to make me gasp.

When he reaches my stomach, he doesn't go straight for my cock. He teases me—lips dragging across the inside of my thigh as he places open-mouthed kisses that make me twitch —before he sucks one of my balls into his mouth, then the other. By the time his mouth hovers over the head of my cock, I'm already shaking and squirming.

"You deserve to be adored," he murmurs as he presses one single kiss to the tip of my cock. "You're the best Christmas gift I've ever received."

And then he sucks me into his mouth, and holy fuck, it's everything. Hot and wet. Pressure and rhythm. The glide of his tongue flicks over my head before he takes me deeper, wrecking me with each suck and stroke. I can't keep still. My hips twitch up, and his hand comes down to hold me there, and it only turns me on more.

The groan that rips out of me is embarrassingly loud, but I can't bring myself to care. Not when he's got me falling apart like this.

"Give me a pillow," Nash says, lifting his head just long enough to speak before taking me back into his mouth.

I grab the one next to me and hand it over, heart pounding. But the second he taps my hips for me to lift up, I hesitate with this gnawing awareness that I'm not ready for more. I hadn't showered since this morning—Sam and I had spent the day together doing everything and nothing, and inviting Nash over was spontaneous. I'm not experienced enough with someone else to not feel self-conscious yet. Not when it comes to this, and I know I need to say something or I won't enjoy myself.

"Nash..." I say quietly, voice a little unsure. "I want to keep going. I really do. Just... not all the way tonight. At least, not unless I've had time to prep better. I'm sorry, I just—"

He pulls off my cock slowly, pressing a kiss to the inside of my thigh like I hadn't just interrupted him.

"That's okay," he murmurs. "Thank you for telling me."

His eyes are looking up at me, but there's no disappointment in them. Just that same softness he always gives me as he brushes his knuckles down my hipbone.

"Do you want to take a shower?" Nash asks.

"Yeah," I say, a little fast. "That'd help."

He smiles, all understanding, and tugs my hand lightly. "Come on, then."

We leave the bed, and somehow, the moment feels just as intimate—maybe even more—as we move into the bathroom. Nash fiddles with the temperature, pulls off his boxer briefs, and looks over his shoulder.

"One second," Nash says, before turning back into the bedroom.

I step into the shower, and a moment later, Nash is there. He wastes no time reaching for the soap, lathering it in his hands before running them down my chest, my arms, my back. He drops his hand lower and gives me a questioning look as his hands start massaging my ass.

The trust I feel with him is unlike any level of trust I've experienced before, so I nod, giving him permission as he begins to rub his soapy fingers over my hole, massaging in circles. When he finally presses in with one finger, my body welcomes him easily, the slickness helping him slide right in.

"Jesus, baby," he groans. "Your hole's eager for me, huh?"

A flush crawls over my skin, but it's not embarrassment this time; it's need. It's want. It's so consuming, I can't swallow it down.

"Yes," I breathe. "More… ready for more."

He slides in a second finger, scissoring them open, then a third. My hips rock into his touch, chasing the pressure, the stretch, the heat. I can't remember what the hesitation felt like earlier because all I feel now is him everywhere.

"I want more," I beg. "Please, Nash."

CHAPTER 28

Nash

I love nothing more than hearing those words leave Caleb's mouth—and everything my baby desires, he gets.

"You want that slutty little hole filled?"

"Yes. Fuck me, Nash. I'm ready," he pants, eyes heavy with lust, hands braced on the wet tile.

"Right here?" I tease, palming his ass. "Or want to go to the bed?"

"Now," he begs. "Here. Please."

That's all I need to hear. I pull my fingers out of him, and push him forward until his chest meets the shower wall. Water slides down his back, pooling in the dips of his spine, and I step in behind him, lining myself up.

"Ass out. Hands on the wall. Keep your back arched for me, just like that," I order. I went back to grab the bottle of lube from the bedside table to bring in here, just in case, and I'm glad I did. "And don't even think about touching yourself until I say so."

He groans, doing exactly as he's told while I rub lube over my cock and his hole, trying to get him ready. I grip his hips and nudge the head of my cock to his entrance. He gasps as I ease in slowly, letting him feel every inch until I'm buried to the hilt. He's tight, warm, and so goddamn perfect. The way he sucks me in makes it nearly impossible to hold back.

Once I'm fully inside him, I pause, letting us both feel it.

"You okay?" I check in, making sure this is still what he wants.

"Fuck," he chokes out, forehead resting against the tile. "So good."

I slide almost all the way out before driving back in, watching the way the muscles in his back tighten with every stroke. His body moves with mine, hips pushing back, greedy for more, and I give him exactly what he wants. The pace builds fast and hard, the slap of our bodies echoes through the steam-filled shower.

"Fucking hell," he cries out. "Fuck, fuck, oh fuck—yes."

I shift one hand from his hip and bring it down on his ass, once, then again, rougher. The sound rips through the space and he moans. My fingers tangle in his soaked hair, tugging just enough to tilt his head back so my mouth can find his ear.

"You take everything I give you so well, baby," I praise. "The way this hole grips me? You were made to take my cock, my perfect little slut."

He whimpers, so far gone now he can barely string words together. Just that need in his voice, that shake in his hands as he braces himself against the wall, tells me everything.

"Please," he grits out. "Fuck."

He's gasping for air, cheeks flushed from the heat and the force of my thrusts, mouth open like he's begging for more, even when he can't find the words as I release his hair.

His back is still arched perfectly, just like I told him, water streaming over every inch of his bare skin. His whole body is rocking forward with every slam of my hips, then jerking back again like he never wants me to leave as he fucks himself on my cock.

My grip tightens on his hips, pulling him harder into me, each thrust slamming home. He sobs out a moan when I shift my angle and hit that spot inside him that makes his knees nearly buckle.

"There," he gasps. "Fuck, Nash—there—right there—"

"You want me to stay right there?" I murmur darkly, leaning over him, lips brushing the shell of his ear. My wet chest is flush against his back, my cock buried so deep he can barely breathe.

"Please—don't stop—don't stop—fuck," he moans.

Moving one hand off his hip, I reach around and palm his throat, not squeezing, just holding and claiming. Caleb's breath hitches, and he whimpers, his dick twitching untouched beneath him, leaking steadily.

"You're mine," I whisper, voice rough and low. "You let me fuck you however I want, don't you? You're *my* slut."

"I'm yours," he pants. "Your slut, Nash. I—fuck—I love when you take me like this."

My cock throbs at the confession, hips stuttering as I slam into him again, even harder now. "Yeah? You love being my hole? That's all you are right now—my perfect hole to use how I please."

I worry it might be too far, but instead, he moans in pleasure. "Yes! Nash, yes," he chokes, pushing back into every thrust like he needs it. "Love being used by you."

I release his throat and wrap my hand around his stomach instead, holding him closely as my thrusts grow erratic. I reach between his legs and brush the slick head of his cock, just once, and he jerks violently.

"Wait, not yet," he cries out. "I'll come too fast."

"Hold it for me then, baby," I growl. "You can do it."

He shudders violently, thighs trembling. "I—I'll try. Feels so good."

I bite down gently on the side of his neck, licking over the temporary mark, loving the way he whimpers beneath me.

"You're doing so good," I grit out. "Taking every inch of me like you were fucking made for it."

His only reply is a desperate moan as I keep thrusting.

"Too close, need to touch you." I gasp, reaching down again, gripping his cock tight and jerking him off in time with my thrusts.

He falls apart: his body tightens, legs shaking uncontrollably, and a strangled cry tears from his throat. "Fuck, Nash, fuck—I'm coming—"

The moment I feel his hole clench around me, I lose it. My grip on his waist turns bruising as I slam into him one last time and come deep inside of him, groaning into the crook of his neck.

We both stand here, panting, bodies trembling from release. My forehead rests against his spine, and his body goes pliant beneath my hands.

I kiss the space between his shoulder blades, still inside him, not ready to be disconnected just yet. Until he shifts, turning around in my arms, and I slip free. He wraps his arms around my neck. His skin's slick and flushed. I hold him close, letting the water rush over both of us while our breathing slows together, and I gently wash him.

When we're finished, I reach past him and turn the water off with one hand and quickly grab two towels from the shelf, wrapping one around his shoulders. My fingers brush along his skin as I pull the towel snug and lean in, kissing him, and he lets out the smallest sigh against my mouth.

I step back, rub the second towel over my arms and chest with quick, practiced movements, then nudge him gently toward the bedroom.

"You doing okay, baby?"

"Yeah, I'm great. Best Christmas ever." Caleb smiles softly.

It's impossible not to smile at that, especially after what he told me a few weeks ago about how Christmas had always felt a bit lonely for him.

Tess was cool when I asked if I could pick the kids up in the morning to bring them here. She's had them all day today, and I told her she could spend the day after with them, too. This way, hopefully everyone gets what they want, and tomorrow is full of everything Caleb and Sam want it to be.

I look back at him now, already curled on his side, watching me.

"Well," I say as I slide into bed, "I'm glad I could help with that. Hopefully, this is the start of a lot of really great Christmases together."

He smiles. "I'd like that. So much, Nash."

I reach for him, pulling him in until we're cuddled up warm and close, his head tucked under my chin. I kiss his forehead, then his temple, then his lips—slow and soft and full of everything I didn't say out loud. I let myself imagine years of this. Holidays and breakfasts and snow days and sleepy nights with tangled legs because I love him, and I want it all. I've hardly known him for a month, but I know in my gut that this is a forever kind of love.

I bury my face into him further, and we stay wrapped up

in each other for a while, but before either of us can fall asleep, I nudge him.

"We should probably go be Santa, huh?" I remind him. I have my gifts for Emma and Benji in the car, and a special one for Caleb that I'll leave in there until tomorrow.

"You're right." He groans as he peels himself out of bed, tugging on a hoodie and a pair of sweats while I do the same, and follow him into the hallway, the soft creak of the wood floor under our feet the only sound.

"So maybe next year, we'll do the gifts before I unwrap you, huh?"

"Probably a smart idea." He laughs.

The living room is dimly lit by the glow of the tree. It's quiet and peaceful and homey—exactly how Christmas Eve should feel.

Caleb crouches by the closet, pulling out the hidden stash of wrapped presents he tucked away in there, and we arrange them under the tree in careful little piles, making sure Sam's name is visible on at least half of them.

"He's gonna lose his mind," Caleb says, smiling down at the gifts like he can already hear Sam's excited shriek.

"He's going to wake us up at the crack of dawn, isn't he?" I ask, which earns me a laugh and a look.

"You know it." Caleb laughs.

I step closer, wrapping my arms around his waist from behind. "Benji is the same way. I'll go pick them up and bring them here as soon as we're awake in the morning, so hopefully Sam doesn't need to wait too long."

He leans into me, his body soft and warm against mine. "Thank you. This is already the best Christmas ever."

We stand there for a minute, just looking at the tree, arms

wrapped around each other until I'm ready to face the cold night.

"I just need to go grab mine from the car. I'll be right back."

"I can help, it'll go quicker, then we can get back into bed sooner," he says with a smirk.

"Well, come on, then." I laugh as we each grab presents from the car and bring them in to set them around Caleb's tree, mixing them with Sam's gifts.

"Alright," he says, standing back and taking a photo of the tree. "We should try to sleep before the tiny tornado shows up."

"True, but we have one more task to do, don't we?" I say, moving toward the kitchen.

"The cookies." He laughs.

Two of the cookies we made earlier are sitting out. One chocolate chip and one sugar cookie, and we each take a bite of one, setting them both back on the plate.

"Is Santa duty complete now?" he asks.

"Sure is, let's go to bed," I say as I kiss his shoulder. I pull him back down the hall, already picturing the way Sam's face will light up in the morning. I'm excited to be here for all of this, and every year after that we're lucky enough to get.

"Merry Christmas, baby," I whisper once we're back in bed.

"Merry Christmas."

CHAPTER 29
Caleb

Nash is still asleep next to me, one arm slung across my waist. I turn my head slightly, watching the way his face softens in sleep. Last night was everything I hoped it would be, and now, waking up with Nash—the person I love —beside me on Christmas day already makes today better than every one before.

From down the hall, I hear the creak of floorboards, and a moment later, there's a soft knock at my bedroom door before Sam opens the door in his fleece pajamas.

"Hey, buddy," I whisper.

"Can I come in?" he asks, already stepping forward.

I nod, and he slips into the room, completely unfazed by seeing Nash in my bed. Sam climbs up into the middle of the bed while Nash shifts to make space without waking up fully —his dad instincts kicking in. He murmurs something that sounds vaguely like "mornin'" and drapes an arm over both of us.

"Santa came! I already checked!" Sam smiles brightly. "Are Benji and Emma coming soon?"

I glance at the clock. "Nash is gonna go pick them up in a little bit."

"Can I go with him?"

"You can if you want, bud," Nash pipes up behind me, his voice still a little raspy from sleep.

"Awesome! It's like having friends over for Christmas!" Sam beams. "I can't wait, then we can all play with our toys!"

I can't help but laugh at the joy radiating off him. My heart feels like it could burst with love. Sam's always loved Christmas, but today he's extra excited, and that's all I wanted for him.

Nash, Benji, and Emma have added so much extra love and joy to our lives, and knowing Sam feels the same makes this change a million times better.

"Well," Nash says, sitting up and stretching, "you think we should check if Santa filled your stocking before we head out?"

"He did!" Sam yells, practically out of the room before Nash finishes his sentence, and I chuckle again.

"Good call on the stocking. That should help him have a little more patience than opening presents," I compliment Nash.

"We can only hope." He smiles back at me as we both get out of bed. Sam's already at the fireplace, and I follow, still grinning as Nash pops into the kitchen to start the coffee. Sam grabs the blue stocking with a snowman on it off the fireplace and starts pulling items out, one by one. He's got candy, a couple of small handheld games, a stocking-sized LEGO set, and a couple more odds and ends.

Nash is watching from the kitchen, leaning against the wall, smiling the entire time, seeing how excited Sam is.

"This is the best Christmas ever," Sam says around a

mouthful of chocolate. "And we haven't even done presents yet!"

Nash catches my eye over the top of Sam's head and mouths, *same.*

I don't say anything back. Just smile and think—*yeah. Same.*

"Alright," Nash says, standing and stretching after Sam's emptied the last of his stocking. "Time to go grab those other two elves."

"I'm coming!" Sam announces, hopping up and rushing to put on his socks.

"You sure you don't mind?" I ask Nash quietly as I rise and walk him to the door.

"Not at all," he says before turning away. "Do you want to come?"

"Nah, it's okay. I'll stay here and get breakfast going so it'll be ready when you all get back."

"Okay, we'll be back soon."

Sam returns, jacket only half zipped. "Let's go!"

Nash gives me a quick kiss before they head out into the cold, and I stand at the window with a fresh cup of coffee, watching the car pull away.

Before I get distracted cooking, I head back to my room and pull out my present for Nash. I'd been so nervous about it because I wanted it to be enough, and I hope he likes it, but it's Nash, so he will.

In the kitchen, I turn on Christmas music, cook the bacon, and pull out what I need to make French toast. The bacon is almost done when I hear the door again, followed by the unmistakable voices of all three kids.

Sam comes barreling into the kitchen. "They're here!"

I bend to let him hug me, and he's still sticky-fingered

from the chocolate in his stocking. Then Benji and Emma come in, red-cheeked from the cold, and I wave them toward the table. Nash trails behind them with a big smile on his face.

"Morning, Caleb," Benji says, eyeing the food with interest.

"Merry Christmas, you two. I've got bacon ready, and the French toast will be done in just a minute."

"Awesome!" Benji grins. "Can we open presents first?"

"How about we eat quick first then we can open presents?" Nash interjects.

"Fineee," Benji whines.

"I'm hungry," Emma adds, sitting on the chair at the table.

Benji and Sam join her, and they look eager to eat, but I know it's just because they want their presents. It's a miracle we're even holding them off this long. Nash helps me finish everything, and we bring the food over to the kids so we can all eat together. I've never had a Christmas like this—with this much laughter and noise. It feels good instead of over-whelming.

When the food is gone and our coffees are refilled, I stand and nod toward the tree.

"Alright," I say. "Presents?"

Sam cheers and Emma squeals while Benji runs over to the tree to start organizing presents by name.

We take our time with it. Each kid opens one gift at a time, torn open with gasps or giggles or a muttered "Whoa, cool," and sometimes a full-blown debate over who gets to play first.

Eventually, they move on to playing with their new gifts, and Nash and I cuddle up on the couch together, watching the scene unfold in front of us like something out of a movie. The room is filled with so much joy, it makes my heart feel like it's going to explode. There's torn wrapping paper everywhere and boxes of toys, and it feels like the five of us are going to start making new traditions.

"I don't think I've ever had a Christmas morning this loud or chaotic," I murmur. "Or perfect. Thank you, Nash. For spending it with us."

"I want to spend every day with you," he says, nudging my shoulder with his. "Let's let them play for a minute. Come to your room with me?"

I nod, standing up from the couch to follow him. When we get to my room, he closes the door behind us. It's still messy from this morning with the bed half made, but neither one of us seems to care.

"Okay," he says, grabbing a present off the dresser that I certainly didn't wrap. "I snuck this in here earlier and was gonna wait till later, but I want you to have it now."

He hands over a small box as I sit on the edge of the bed and open it slowly. Inside is a photo. One I didn't know he had or one that was ever taken.

It's the picture of us on the day we made cinnamon rolls. I'm mid-laugh, and Nash is looking at me with so much love in his eyes.

"Flip it over."

I do, and see something written on the back of it: *You didn't just change my life, Caleb. You've helped me see my forever.*

My throat tightens. I blink a few times before looking up. "Nash…"

"I wanted you to have something to keep with you. Even when we're apart," he says before leaning in to kiss me.

"This is the best gift I've ever gotten, thank you." I

swallow the lump in my throat and reach for his gift. It's wrapped in the only paper I had left—blue with candy canes—and sealed with an uneven line of tape. "Your turn."

He smiles, then starts peeling back the paper. When he gets the top off the box, he pauses, mouth twitching into a smile.

Inside is a set of matching pajamas—red and black plaid flannel pants and soft thermal shirts, one in his size, one in mine.

"Caleb! These are perfect," he exclaims, a little surprised.

"You said you wanted matching pajamas, so I got them for us. The kids too, if you don't think that's overboard. They're just in a separate box I hadn't given them yet."

"Absolutely. We're all wearing them, baby. Thank you for doing this!"

He huffs a laugh, still staring at the gift, like it was truly a big thing.

"There's a note at the bottom," I say.

He lifts the pajamas and pulls out the folded scrap of paper I tucked under them.

I never thought I'd get to have this with someone. I'm glad it's you.

When he looks up again, his eyes are suspiciously shiny. "Caleb."

"Yeah?"

"I love you."

There's no build up or big speech; he just says it like it's an absolute truth.

"I love you too, Nash. So much."

He leans in and captures my mouth with his, sealing the words between us. When we finally pull apart, I press my forehead to his, breathing him in.

"We should probably go back out there," I murmur. "Before they tear the house down."

"Five more seconds," he whispers, arms tightening around my waist. "Just want more time with you."

"Mmm," I agree, eyes closed, soaking up the warmth of his body against mine.

Eventually, we break apart and start pulling on our matching pajamas.

"Let's take a photo in the mirror." Nash grins, holding up his phone, and I absolutely go along with it because he looks too damn happy not to.

"Speaking of photos," I say as we pose, "when did you get the one of us in the kitchen at your house?"

"When you ran to the bathroom, I gave Sam my phone and asked him to take a couple of pictures of us when you weren't looking," he says casually, like he didn't just admit to the cutest thing ever.

"Huh, I hadn't even noticed. But I love that you thought of it."

We grin in the mirror, and Nash is wrapped around me, his chin tucked over my shoulder as he takes the photo.

"Let's go give the kids theirs," I say. "I have their box under my bed."

He grabs my hand before we leave the room, lacing our fingers together.

"This is the life I want, you know," I admit quietly. "Messy and loud and full of the kids and you."

He squeezes my hand. "I'm not going anywhere, baby. I love you."

We walk back out into the living room, and Emma sees it first.

"Another present?" She gasps excitedly.

"What is it?" Benji adds on.

"Open it and see," Nash says, dropping onto the couch and tugging me down with him.

They dig in fast, and the shrieks of laughter that follow are so pure it makes my chest ache.

"Pajamas!" Benji says, holding up a pair.

"Do we all match?" Sam asks, looking between me and Nash.

I nod. "Yep. Full-on corny family Christmas vibe. Go change, we can take a photo in front of the tree."

The kids scatter, each grabbing their set and disappearing down the hall.

Nash leans in close, voice low against my ear. "We are so those people now."

I laugh, leaning into him. "You say that like it's a bad thing."

"Not even a little. This was my idea, after all."

Not even a minute later, Sam and Benji come running back into the living room before Emma joins.

"Okay, everyone," I say, grabbing my phone. "In front of the tree. Nash, let's figure out where to put your phone."

He sets it up on some books and starts the timer. "Ten seconds!"

I'm sitting on the floor, and Nash settles behind me, one arm slung around my chest as the kids pile in close.

The shutter clicks as the timer goes off.

And when Nash shows me, it's perfect.

I know, right then, that I've found the perfect man who will give me everything I want, like it's second nature. He sees all of me and doesn't flinch, and he seamlessly fits into the mess of my life like he was always meant to be here. He's the steady I didn't think I'd ever get to have. He gives without keeping score. He kisses me like he's still in awe that he gets to. He makes me laugh more than I've laughed in a long time. He makes the weight I've been carrying feel lighter just by sharing the space.

And the thing is, I didn't even know how much I needed all of that until he gave it to me.

I've given my sexuality more thought over the last couple of days, and honestly, I'm still figuring it out. Maybe I'm gay and not bi, but the label doesn't matter as much to me as this truth: I'm in love with a man.

A man who makes me feel more seen, more wanted, and more myself than anyone else in the world.

All that matters is that he loves me and my son like he was always destined for us.

He's my forever.

Epilogue: Nash
ONE YEAR LATER

B eing back at the ski resort in December sparks so many happy memories. This time it's just Caleb and me, though. My partner, my person, the best thing I've ever found waiting in a ski line.

Tess and her boyfriend of the last seven months or so have all three kids for the weekend, and we couldn't have asked for a better co-parenting setup. She's been more than accommodating, making space for Sam like he's always belonged, and easing some of that unspoken worry Caleb carried about blending our families.

Not everyone has shown that same acceptance, though. When Caleb came out to his parents this spring, their reaction went about how he expected. They didn't take it well, but instead of letting it crush him, it finally gave him clarity.

He realized how much hiding had given them control. For years, he shaped his life to avoid conflict, always trying to make everyone else happy while carrying the weight of their expectations. Finally saying the words out loud stripped that power away. Losing them hurt, but hiding had cost him far more.

That's when he understood that freedom isn't about who accepts you. It's about learning to accept yourself.

He also proudly labeled himself gay.

To say I'm proud of him is an understatement.

Over the summer, Sam and Caleb moved into our house. It may seem quick to most people, but for us, it's never felt that way. It just felt right. Ever since we went all in December of last year, we'd known this was it. Sam's settled into school with Emma and Benji, and the three of them are thick as thieves.

Now, Caleb is standing a few feet ahead of me on his skis, adjusting his gloves, the tip of his nose already pink from the cold. His goggles are pushed up on his helmet as he gets ready to get in the lift line.

"You ready?" I ask, nudging him gently as I slide up next to him.

"I've had two coffees and two Tylenol. That's as ready as I can be." He laughs.

God, I love him.

We ride the lift up and spend the morning taking slow runs since we don't have the kids to chase down the mountain. By midday, we're both worn out and cold. Caleb glides to a stop beside me at the base, cheeks flushed under his helmet, breath puffing in little white clouds. He flips up his goggles. "One more run then lunch?"

I nod, hoping he can't hear how hard my heart is pounding. "You read my mind," I say, aiming for casual, even though I've been nervously waiting for this all day.

He falls into place beside me in the lift line and smiles up at me. The chair lift brings us back up the mountain, and my nerves are on fire as my fingers toy with the edge of the ring box hidden in my coat.

We've discussed remarrying a few times, and Caleb has been vocal about wanting to get married again "one day." And I want to show him how good marriage can be with the right person.

"Follow me," I say to Caleb once we get off, skiing toward a perfect slice of solitude that sits off the main run. It's a little pull-off with a bench and a stunning overlook with unobstructed views. It's the perfect place to ask him to spend forever with me. When we ski over, I unclip my skis and take off my helmet and goggles. Caleb does the same, looking at me, confused.

His brows lift, curious. "What are you—"

I take that chance to step in front of him, reaching into the inside pocket of my coat to pull out the box and dropping down to one knee.

"The mountains have always been a special place for us," I start. "This is the place I met you, and the place my whole life rerouted because of one conversation in the lift line."

His eyes soften at my speech.

"You let Benji and me jump on the lift with you, crash your lunch at the lodge, and let me hold you the very first night in a room you definitely weren't planning to share. That one day changed my entire life for the better, and I knew I'd never get enough of you. You gave me something I didn't know I'd been missing, Cay, and I never want to let you go."

His eyes are wide, and he's grinning so big watching me. I open the box and show him the simple silver band inside.

"Will you marry me, Caleb?"

He exhales a shaky laugh that melts straight into a smile.

"Yes," he exclaims, voice thick with emotion. "Yes, I want to marry you!"

Before I can even slide the ring on, he grabs my jacket and pulls me up and into him. Our mouths crash together, and he kisses me with everything he's got.

When we finally pull apart, both of us breathless, I take his hand in mine. His gloves are already off, and I slide the ring onto his bare finger.

"I love you," he says, still a little breathless.

I press my forehead to his. "I love you too. So damn much."

We ski back down the mountain and head to our hotel room—the same resort we first got snowed in at, except this time we have a king-bed suite to celebrate in all by ourselves.

Because this isn't just where we started.

It's where we both found our forever.

THE END.

Bonus Chapter

Loved Caleb and Nash?

Read about New Year's Eve right after Caleb and Nash get engaged. It's *double* the fun.

Get the bonus chapter here: https://becbenson.com/all-in-december

It's the perfect final scene to wrap up their story... and start the new year right.

Acknowledgments

Thank you to all my beta readers: Lys, Marco, Rod, Nati, Jonathan, Bryoni, Em, and Jenny. You all helped shape this book with your feedback! Toddles, thank you for helping me bring this book over the finish line!

Thank you, Amimbia, for the stunning cover art! It's so beautiful.

Thank you, Lexi, for encouraging me to write this book (once again). I wouldn't know what to do without you on this author journey.

Colorado will always and forever hold a special place in my heart, and writing this was a reminder of just how much I love the mountains in December and all the magic they can bring.

About the Author

Bec Benson is based in the Northeast, lives for the first sip of hot coffee in the morning, genuinely believes emo music can make you happy, and is obsessed with mgk.

Come hang out in **Lexi Amber and Bec Benson's Romance Readers** here: https://www.facebook.com/groups/lexiandbec

Also by Bec Benson

Straight to You

Co-written with Lexi Amber:

The Reality of Wanting Him

The Reality of Wanting My Bully